THE

CORRUPTION

OF

PHILIP TOLES

A NOVEL

BY FELIX I.D. DIMARO

THE CORRUPTION
OF
PHILIP TOLES

Written by FELIX I.D. DIMARO

Cover Artwork: Rosco Nischler
Interior Artwork: Rosco Nischler
Typography and Graphic Design: Courtney Swank
Editor: Alessandra Sztrimbely

Copyright © 2021 by Felix I.D. Dimaro

ALSO BY FELIX I.D. DIMARO

How To Make A Monster
The Loveliest Shade of Red

BUG SPRAY
A Tale of ~~Love and~~ Madness

VIRAL LIVES
A Ghost Story

2222

THE FIRE ON MEMORY LANE

Warning

This story contains mature subject matter, including coarse language, references to suicide, child abuse, child predation, and scenes depicting graphic violence.

Discretion is advised.

For the Good Kids... And for the kids who never got the chance to be

"The true character of a society is revealed in how it treats its children."

Nelson Mandela

PART ONE

STUDENT BODY

ONE bad October morning resulted in the ruin of so many lives.

At eight fifteen a.m., on Wednesday October sixteenth, before first period gym class was to begin at Rosenthal P. Straily Public School, Philip Alexander Toles – an eighth-grade student who should have been celebrating his thirteenth birthday – was found dead. Hanging by the neck from a rope attached to one of the many basketball hoops in the school's gymnasium, a painter's ladder overturned on the floor beneath him. Beside that ladder was a cap. A red baseball cap. The same red baseball cap Philip was nearly never seen without.

Gym class, of course, was cancelled that morning. As was the rest of the school day. Despondent students lingered around the school grounds, thankful for the day off from classes but not sure what to make of what had happened to their classmate. Some made fun of the suicide, hearing from their parents that those who committed the act were damned, not to be mourned. Others huddled in groups, suddenly and jarringly reminded of the mortality that, to youth of that age, seems like a thing one might never have to be concerned with. Some tried desperately to understand how someone so young and so well-liked could come to the decision of suicide, while others understood the decision completely. These latter children, even amidst the mourning (or perhaps encouraged by it) thought of committing the act themselves.

After most of those confused and concerned students had cleared the grounds, the teachers, equally as despondent as those students, gathered in their lounge. An impromptu staff meeting was held to discuss how things would be handled, to figure out how to move forward.

The gym teacher who had discovered the boy's body before her first period class was sitting quietly. One of many who seemed to have temporarily forgotten how to turn emotion into thought and thought into speech. Even when she could find a word or two in the fog of sadness that was her thoughts, none of those words seemed right. None of them felt good enough. Not in this situation that made no sense to her. To anyone around her.

One of the reasons so many of the teachers were silent was the result of one teacher's noise. One teacher who went from questioning "Why?" repeatedly and in a variety of ways, to crying, nearly wailing, mourning the boy as though he were her son. Several focused their efforts on consoling her. Those people were thankful for the distraction, for this vacuum of grief to allow them something to concentrate on. Something to heal and nurture. Others, however, looked at Mrs. Kathleen Jeffreys, the seventh and eighth grade social studies teacher, with a skeptical eye. Hers seemed to be an extreme reaction, even for this situation.

In the silences between Mrs. Jeffreys' wails, the wall clock could be heard loudly ticking away the seconds, seemingly ten minutes at a time. When it felt as though they had been there for a day or more (though the clock indicated it was only a few minutes past eleven a.m.), and

The Corruption of Philip Toles

as Mrs. Jeffreys wailed and was comforted and was looked upon with skepticism, there was a knock on the door.

The door was answered. No one was too surprised to see the two police officers standing there, politely asking to enter. The police had been there all morning, and the teachers understood this interruption. A death had occurred. Information had to be gathered. Reports had to be filed. But that was not why these officers were here. These officers had not arrived to obtain information, but to provide it. And they had several things to say to one specific person.

This already disturbing day became more bewildering when the police asked for Mrs. Kathleen Jeffreys in particular. Everyone looked to the woman, who now not only appeared bereaved but also afraid. With the presence of law enforcement in the room, some started to believe she even looked guilty. The police certainly seemed to think so as they carefully brought the woman to her feet, put her in handcuffs, and let her know just why she was being placed inside those shackles.

They spoke to Kathleen specifically, though their words would forever be remembered by all inside the lounge. Words that would change their lives, the school, the community, many futures.

"Kathleen Jeffreys. You're under arrest for..." The officer had to pause to compose himself. Began reading from a piece of paper. A list. Each item he named adding to the horror of the day. The words he read were:

Sexual interference.

Sexual exploitation.

Invitation to sexual touching.

Aggravated sexual assault of a child.

Unlawful sex with a minor.

Continuous sexual abuse of a child.

5

Conspiracy to commit kidnapping.

Online corruption of a minor.

Kathleen Jeffreys was hauled away still wailing and mourning, accused of being responsible for the corruption of Philip Toles. And his death as a result of it.

If I don't do this I'll be stuck in this shitty town and school forever.

If I don't do this I'll never be happy.

If I don't do this I'll never be free.

I think my mom hates me, maybe she'll be happy when I'm gone.

Mrs Jeffreys made me so many promises, If I do this she'll feel bad about that.

TWO months after the death of Philip Toles, the

fervor and frenzy surrounding the boy's demise and what
the newspapers were calling 'the affair' between a male
student and female teacher had yet to die down.

Mr. Morris Corbray, the school's guidance counsellor,
personally hated that term. 'The affair'. He and many other
members of the staff, both male and female, had considered
how the media would have likely reported the situation had
it been a male teacher with a student. All of them, each
former friend and co-worker of the now fired Kathleen
Jeffreys, hoped she wouldn't be let off with a slap on the
wrist, which was often the case in situations like this.
Though the fact that the boy had died, and had left behind
a note with her name on it in the pocket of the jeans he had
died in, made Mrs. Jeffreys' situation a dire one. It had
certainly made the lives of the entire staff at the school
increasingly difficult. No one's more so than Mr. Corbray's.

Mr. Corbray had not been present in the teacher's
lounge during Mrs. Jeffreys' arrest. He had instead been
doing damage control from the moment the child's body
had been discovered. On that October morning, he had
been sitting in his office while children who were too afraid
to go home, too confused to know what to do with

themselves, lined up to enter his office and receive guidance from their counsellor. It had been nonstop ever since. The teachers were still scrambling. The kids weren't alright.

This was another of those nonstop days. Mr. Corbray sat at his desk eating a bagged lunch and looking at something in front of him that he refused to believe. He took a bite of his turkey sandwich, a piece of onion falling onto the newspaper on his desk. He brushed it off and saw the oil from the onion stain the newsprint, like the news in the paper would continue to stain their lives.

He had first seen the headline when he had grabbed the newspaper from the lounge that morning, though because he'd been running late, he hadn't had a chance to read it. Even now he barely had time to do so. His last appointment – an eleven-year-old boy whose grades were suffering because his parents were going through a divorce – had run into his lunchtime. He always brought a bagged lunch these days, mainly to avoid having to enter the cafeteria. Since Philip's death, Mr. Corbray had nearly no alone time during schooldays. Teachers and students seemed to constantly want to chat with him when they saw him in the lunchroom or hallways, usually asking for an update on the case or for general advice. Even after school, during what should have been his free time, his life had become full of constant human interaction.

Mr. Corbray had been Philip's counsellor. Had sat with the boy at least once a week, helping him through his many issues at home, including dealing with a dead father and distant mother. He had grown very close to Philip, and had been devastated by the news of the relationship between the boy and Mr. Corbray's colleague and friend, Kathleen Jeffreys. He missed Philip terribly even now, though he had to maintain his composure, particularly since he had somehow become so integral to this entire situation.

Because of his relationship with both Mrs. Jeffreys and Philip Toles, Mr. Corbray had been contacted by several news outlets for his opinion on the matter. His school – its reputation – was in trouble, and he had somehow become the spokesperson, the representative voice of Rosenthal P. Straily Public School. This position as representative had come with a great deal of work and pressure, especially considering the school was named after a founding father of the city of Saturn, a borough nestled beside the city of Toronto, in Ontario, Canada. Because of the school's historical relevance, based on its name and the fact that it was one of the oldest educational institutions in the city, Rosenthal P. Straily P.S. was always supposed to shine brighter, to be held to a higher standard, than other elementary schools in the region.

Tension. Stress. This was Morris Corbray's life.

To make matters worse, he was likely to be called as a witness for the prosecution against Mrs. Jeffreys at her preliminary hearing in the upcoming months, which meant he had to be especially careful about what he said to the media and his peers prior to the case going to court. He did not want to contradict himself or appear unreliable when it came time to give his official testimony.

The counsellor, the friend, the witness, Mr. Corbray's face was in newspapers, on the internet. Everywhere. His quotes asking for reason and peace and healing had, on one occasion, started off the local morning news. That newscast had gone on to show footage of protests outside the court where most cases of this nature were tried in Saturn City. The protesters gathered outside the court despite Kathleen Jeffreys not being there. Despite her not yet having a court date. They gathered there *because* she was not there to be tried, nor was she in jail. These people were protesting not only Kathleen's crime, her existence, but also the fact that she was allowed to be free while awaiting her day in court. This did not sit well with the community.

Now, reading this morning's edition of the Saturn Sun, Mr. Corbray understood why Kathleen would remain free until whenever a trial date was set. He wondered what the reaction to this new news would be, knowing it wouldn't be positive. Far from it. He only hoped that nothing, including the school itself, would burn thanks to this new development.

There had already been a few small protests outside of R.P. Straily P.S.; parents and caring community members demanding the resignation of the principal and superintendent, the mistreatment and death of a child having occurred on their watch. Mr. Corbray had been there, putting out fires, helping to bring calm. He was a well appreciated man, and though he appreciated being appreciated, he was far too in the center of it all for his liking.

The news he was reading now – news that had nothing to do with him at all – wasn't going to help remove him or his coworkers from the center of things. The school was about to be in a firestorm, figuratively speaking if not literally. Again. Or, more accurately, additional fuel had been flung onto the inferno they were already in the middle of. Things were going to get hotter, and they were going to get hotter immediately.

Mr. Corbray had ignored his office phone all morning because he had seen the headline and had known what to expect. Now he had a plethora of voicemails on his answering machine, likely from reporters looking for insight on this development to the story.

An hour prior, due to the fact that he had been ignoring his phone for much of the morning, the school's secretary had knocked on his door, interrupting his session to tell him that there was to be an emergency meeting after school. He had known it would be about this. This dismal news in front of him.

Checking the time, he folded up the newspaper and went to put it away, taking one final glance at the front page. Above two side-by-side photos – one of Philip Toles, one of Kathleen Jeffreys – was the headline:

TEACHER ARRESTED FOR INVOLVEMENT WITH STUDENT CONFIRMS PREGNANCY

Mrs. Jeffreys was with child, and four months along at that. The article indicated that she was considering entering a guilty plea instead of continuing to maintain her innocence. With a baby now involved, the disgraced educator was looking to avoid a lengthy court proceeding. She wanted a shorter sentence, a faster release, and, she hoped, a chance to live a life with her and Philip's child.

Mr. Corbray shook his head, hoping she would get none of those things. The guidance counsellor put the paper in his desk drawer. He took a deep breath, attempting to mentally prepare himself for what was going to be a hectic afternoon. And for the storm they were sure to be in until Kathleen Jeffreys was finally convicted and sentenced.

"THREE years? Are you kidding me? Only *three years!* What a fucking joke, your *honour!*" This was Solomon Toles, grandfather of Philip.

Mr. Corbray, other staff members from the school, and many members of the community were currently inside of a courtroom listening to Solomon admonish a judge.

This was a little over a year after Philip Toles had died. More accurately, it was a year and two weeks after the note implicating his social studies teacher in multiple crimes had been discovered in his pocket. The discovery of that note had led to a thorough investigation into the email interactions between Philip and Mrs. Jeffreys, and the revelation that the two had exchanged more than five hundred electronic messages over a period of ten months, starting when Philip had been a twelve-year-old seventh grader enrolled in Mrs. Jeffreys' social studies class. Many of the emails were of an explicit and sexual nature.

Even with all the evidence against her, Kathleen Jeffreys had managed to cut a deal; a plea of guilty in exchange for certain charges being dropped, as well as a sentence she and her lawyers found reasonable. Short of her immediate freedom, she had gotten essentially what she had hoped for.

The judge had just announced to the court that this grown woman, this educator and caregiver who had taken advantage of a vulnerable minor, who had taken his virginity, ruined his life, and was the reason for his death, was only going to go to prison for three years. She might be out in less time than that depending on her behaviour.

There was uproar. There was outrage.

Once Solomon had exploded at the judge, others had followed suit and voiced their complaints, vented their anger.

The gavel banged against the judge's bench.

Order was asked for. Order was not restored.

Not for some time. Not until the older gentleman gave the judge, the bailiff, the entire court, one more reproachful look. His eyes lingered on Kathleen Jeffreys, who was sitting there with her defense team, not looking back at Philip's grandfather.

"You'll get your justice in Hell, you raping whore!" Solomon screamed. More noise and racket followed this.

Grandfather Toles stormed out of the courtroom, but not before he made eye contact with Mr. Corbray, who was observing it all quietly in the audience. Solomon gave the guidance counsellor a sorrowful and knowing glance before his exit.

They had discussed this, is what that look said. They both knew this was how it was going to go. Mr. Corbray returned Solomon's expression.

Philip's grandfather was only two years older than the guidance counsellor, though most wouldn't have guessed they were in the same age bracket. Seeing him here today, Mr. Corbray realized that Solomon looked nearly a decade older than his fifty-four years. Older than the last time he and Mr. Corbray had seen each other.

That had been back in March when Solomon had asked the guidance counsellor to meet him for lunch. That was two months before Mrs. Jeffreys had been due to give birth, and roughly seven months before this day. It turned out that she had been nearly two months pregnant when Philip had died.

Everyone eager for this case to be resolved had been made to wait until the baby's birth before proceedings were resumed against Mrs. Jeffreys, even though she had pled guilty. The judge had pushed back the date of the sentencing for the sake of the baby. He had stated that the stress of the ongoing proceedings might be detrimental to the unborn child's health. The community had been incensed. The salacious teacher would be free longer, unpunished for a greater duration of time, resting comfortably while Philip turned to bones in a box in the ground.

Mr. Corbray knew that if Solomon (or any of the others currently creating a ruckus in the court or eagerly awaiting news of the sentencing in the community) had had it his way, this would have been treated as a murder trial, and Mrs. Jeffreys would be facing life behind bars.

If asked for honesty, many would have admitted to preferring something akin to a witch trial. Mrs. Jeffreys tied to a stake and burning. Instead, the people were watching what seemed to be a system that was eager to put a child abuser, manipulator, predator, rapist back on the street as quickly as could be justified. And this could barely be justified, Mr. Corbray thought. He understood the uproar, the outrage. But he didn't participate in it because he was unsurprised.

When Solomon had asked the counsellor to join him for a drink and a discussion over lunch back in March, Mr. Corbray had been nervous, even scared, that Philip's grandfather would blame him for Philip's demise. Would hold Mr. Corbray, one of the educators who let his grandson down, responsible. He wouldn't have been the first.

Much of the anger regarding the scandal had been directed at the school. The staff at R.P. Straily had become the next logical target for the protestors after Kathleen was relocated and her family, though they'd had nothing to do with her perversity, chased out of town.

A family that included a husband, two daughters.

It turned out that Kathleen's pregnancy was what Solomon had wanted to speak to Mr. Corbray about. He wanted to discuss her baby, and his frustration over the fact that he wouldn't be able to adopt it. He also wanted to discuss the possibility that Kathleen might be allowed to keep the child after her prison sentence was over.

That was the talk of the town.

When the news of her pregnancy had first been announced, attention had turned to Kathleen's husband, no one wanting to believe her insistence that the baby was Philip's. Her husband, however, quickly stated that they had been fighting for months prior to her arrest. And had not been intimate during that time. She'd been a neglectful wife and mother, her husband had said. Then had gone as far as to say he hadn't been shocked to find out about the affair. Nor was he surprised when it was uncovered, through Philip's note and his email interactions with his social studies teacher, that the woman had been planning to leave town with the boy. To 'start a new life'. Her pregnancy had been the main motivating factor in her decision to flee and take Philip with her.

During their lunch, Mr. Corbray had assured Solomon, as they watched a pair of beers go flat and appetizers grow cold on the table between them, that Kathleen's uncovered plan to abandon her existing children would weigh heavily against her chance of maintaining her parental rights to this new child. But Solomon hadn't been convinced.

In response to Mr. Corbray's assurances, Solomon had reached beside him into a faded brown leather satchel he had brought with him to the restaurant. The bag looked as if it were something the aging man might have owned since boyhood. Solomon withdrew from it a folder. Opened the folder and placed its contents on the table for both men to see. They were looking at printed news stories, articles he had found online about female teachers who had raped young boys in the past. What he highlighted for Mr. Corbray was disheartening, though not unexpected.

The two men had gone through several stories, all involving women similar to Kathleen: Caucasian, slowly approaching the void of middle age, most of them married, many of them parents, all of them having sex for months, if not years, with boys barely into puberty.

What these stories also had in common was the fact that the perpetrators often received a slap on the wrist. If that. For these teachers – these boy-seducers, child rapists who had been caught red handed, caught, as Kathleen had been, with hundreds of email interactions, with notes passed back and forth, with admissions of 'love' from both parties – it wasn't uncommon for them to receive zero jail time.

Often, it was probation. In some cases, they were permitted to go back to teaching as though the violation of these boys hadn't mattered. As though, because the young boys' bodies may have enjoyed the act, it had had no effect on their minds. Their psyches. As though their very selves weren't being corrupted with each touch, each lie, each manipulation from an adult they were supposed to be able to trust.

Among these news reports was the infamous case of Mary Kay Letourneau, an American teacher who had married her former sixth-grade student after she had been imprisoned for raping him. After he impregnated her. The teacher and student wound up raising two children together once the supposed justice system had had its say.

"That's what can't happen," Solomon had said when they looked over the documents regarding the Letourneau case. "I can't have it so Jeffreys goes to prison, does a light stretch, and then comes out and takes my great-grandchild."

He'd said 'take', Corbray had noted. And he wondered if Solomon held onto some sort of genuine hope of adopting the child. From what Mr. Corbray knew of the Toles family, it was unlikely to happen. But not because Solomon himself had any issues. In fact, he was an upstanding small business owner – a locksmith three provinces west, in Alberta.

Solomon had left his business in the hands of a trusted apprentice and had rushed to Saturn City upon hearing of Philip's death. Had moved in with Philip's mother, Amanda Toles, to help take some of the burden of grief from her, in hopes that they could share this sorrow together. Which they had. Until Philip's mother had suddenly taken off one day.

Amanda had been dating someone during the last year of Philip's life, if you could call an online relationship with a stranger in Texas 'dating'. It seemed, with Philip dead, his mother felt she no longer had to stay in Saturn. According to Solomon, on one morning, only weeks after Philip's funeral (one of the saddest and most sorrowful ceremonies Mr. Corbray had ever attended), Amanda had just up and left the country and her old life behind to live with her online boyfriend. A man she had said would 'take care of her'.

Mr. Corbray hadn't been shocked to learn about the departure of Amanda Toles. Her indifference to, and borderline neglect of, her son had been what had brought Philip to Mr. Corbray in the first place. The boy had been desperate for an adult to provide him guidance, to show him he could be cared for and nurtured. His grandfather, the only positive adult influence in Philip's life, had only been able to see him on special occasions due to Solomon's hectic and relentless schedule as the sole owner of a business.

When Amanda had left for Texas, not only had she left the burden of grief with her father-in-law, she had also left behind her apartment and most of her belongings. Despite how much his daughter-in-law leaving him and everything behind had hurt Solomon, what had truly broken his heart was what Philip's mother had taken with her. With her, she had taken any chance of Solomon being able to adopt Philip's child. He was a single, aging man from another province who had to work around the clock daily in order to keep his business afloat. Amanda Toles may not have gone to Texas with many belongings in tow, but somehow, to Solomon, she had taken everything that mattered to him with her.

While the fact that he was alone, from another province, and a male, wouldn't help Solomon's case when it came to adopting Philip's child, Mr. Corbray knew there was a more pertinent reason the child of Kathleen and Philip wouldn't be given to Solomon.

Although Philip was a Caucasian boy, Solomon was a Black man. To be more accurate, he was a man of mixed race. He had extremely light brown skin, green eyes, curly copper coloured hair (where it hadn't begun to grey), and a smattering of light brown freckles across his nose and cheeks. At a glance, he could pass for a tanned white man. Still, regardless of his white genes and white features, the world, and those who ran it, would always consider him to be Black. Mr. Corbray had been around the system long enough to know that there was no way a white child would be awarded to an old single Black man. As unfair as it seemed, this was simply the way things were.

Mr. Corbray hadn't known how to say plainly to Solomon that it would be the foster system that would claim his great-grandchild, so he had steered the conversation back toward the verdict and Kathleen Jeffreys herself instead.

At the end of a lunch where not a single bite of food had been consumed, Solomon had said he was hoping the justice system would do what it had failed to do so many times before. To actually get a morally corrupt person, a person who corrupted others morally, off the streets, out of the schools, and locked away.

Mr. Corbray had vehemently agreed.

Now, in the courtroom, months after the baby had been born, as the judge and his gavel were being ignored, Mr. Corbray looked over at Mrs. Jeffreys, crying and carrying on, hugging her defense attorney. He couldn't quite determine if she was sad about the verdict or celebrating it. But he knew she should feel lucky either way.

He resented her deeply. Resented what she had done to him. To Philip. To the order they had all once enjoyed in their lives. He knew, though, despite the verdict, that the woman couldn't possibly be happy. Her baby was already in the foster system, as Mr. Corbray had expected, and there was no guarantee she would ever get the child back. That was the real punishment. A punishment for this woman and, potentially, unfortunately, for the child. Mr. Corbray was well aware that the foster system was full of all sorts of sickos and bad influences and pitfalls that could ruin a child. Many of his favourite students came from that system. He knew it well. Knew its dangers.

The Corruption of Philip Toles

After the crowd in the court began to settle, the judge continued on with the sentencing, reading the full terms that Kathleen Jeffreys would have to abide by for the years following her release from prison.

She would have to register as a sex offender and would no longer be allowed to teach; she would not be allowed to travel without receiving permission from the courts, her internet access would be restricted, and she would have to report to a parole officer for a minimum of five years after she was released.

Terms. Conditions. All the crowd heard was a blathering judge announcing that this predatory woman would soon be free. Would be able to one day start a new life, and might still have a chance to be part of her child's life after some years, and after meeting other conditions, which had yet to be settled upon.

It sounded like an easy ride for a privileged pedophile.

The crowd began to grow hostile again.

Mr. Corbray once more wondered if he had failed. He thought back to his testimony against Kathleen during the preliminary hearing, before she had decided to give up her defense and plead guilty for a lesser sentence. What more could he have said? How much more could he have influenced the court? He had made clear to the judge how dangerous she was. He had specifically mentioned in his testimony the fact that Philip had confided in him about being smitten with an older girl during the months leading up to his death. Mr. Corbray had assumed that Philip's crush had been an older classmate or some girl from the neighbourhood. Looking back, he could see how that 'older girl' – who he would later understand was Kathleen Jeffreys – had changed the boy. Dimmed him.

Mr. Corbray had stated in no uncertain terms that other children would always be at risk if someone like Kathleen

Jeffreys were allowed to go free without extensive jailtime and proper rehabilitation. He knew now that she would be receiving neither of these things.

Mr. Corbray, feeling partially responsible for all of this, simply shook his head and left the courtroom. He prepared himself for the media persons who were bound to bombard him with questions the moment he exited the building.

Walking toward that bombardment, he wondered how the rest of the city would respond to the news of this sentencing.

FOUR hours left. Just four more hours to go, Jabari Henry said to himself a few minutes after finishing with his last client and while waiting for the next. It was the morning shift. The shift which seemed to stretch out the longest. The one that always made eight hours feel like twelve. The shift that made the day seem to last forever, even before he got to work.

He had to be awake before five a.m., ready for pick up at six in order to be driven out to one of several worksites, each usually an hour away from the condo unit he shared with his roommate and best friend in Central Saturn.

Most of the worksites were comfortable at least, including today's location. Jabari couldn't complain about that. What he disliked about the shift was the inconsistency. Because clients usually came in to see him before they started their workday or during their lunch breaks, it was bursts of go, go, go interspersed with long stretches of waiting for the clock to move faster.

He wanted his shift to be over entirely so he could fully immerse himself in what had unfolded that morning. What was still unfolding even now. The entire day, he had been learning of the events in bits and pieces, listening to his iPod for updates whenever he had a break. He was currently looking forward to this next stretch of nothing to do and no one to service because of what he badly wanted to go back to listening to. His body reminded him that it was time to eat, but he ignored the hunger pangs, as he always did before and during his shifts. As he often did throughout most of his days. Sitting down at his small, anachronistic roll-top desk, he put an ear bud in his left ear, leaving the right bud dangling and that ear free to hear the site boss or any potential clients who came knocking on the door.

His iPod was tuned to the rarely used radio function, set to a local news station. Listening to the news was not his usual leisurely time-killing activity. He typically listened to music to pass the time. Tuning in to the news was a fairly new habit of his. One he had started since hearing about the case of the boy who had been found hanging at Jabari's old elementary school.

Jabari had become particularly interested in the case after he had heard the name of the teacher accused. Mrs. Kathleen Jeffreys, his former social studies teacher. He had been following the story raptly ever since. The wild unexpected twist with the pregnancy, the statements given by the principal, the guidance counsellor and others. It was better than the reality TV shows everyone seemed to be obsessed with these days. Especially since, only four years earlier, he had been walking through those elementary school halls. He felt like he was almost a part of the story. And he had good reason to feel this way. Though he had never met Philip (Jabari was four years his senior), he could relate to the dead boy's experience with the faculty at R.P. Straily. He was reminded of his own experience at the school when he first saw several of the faculty members on the news once the story of Philip's death broke.

The Corruption of Philip Toles

It wasn't often you saw on the news the person who had given you your first blowjob. Especially not when that person was an adult, and an authority figure.

Attempting to catch up on the case now, Jabari had to sit through a newsflash update which teased the full details of the court's announcement as well as a listing of sporting events that would be going on that night in Saturn and neighbouring Toronto. Then came an advertisement for mattresses he had listened to so many times he hummed along to it. Eventually, he heard the full update on the sentencing.

"Three years... She only got three years," Jabari said, then whistled. *People are going to be pissed*, he thought. Most were hoping she would get a minimum of ten years. Jabari, however, was unsurprised, and began to laugh as he heard the clips of people giving their thoughts on the matter, including that of his genuinely upset sounding former guidance counsellor, Mr. Corbray. So many people hurt because they had expected too much of society. He laughed again, thinking to himself, *If they only knew*.

But he knew. Jabari had knowledge of certain things. Had information, and information was valuable. At least that's what his manager, Bruna, always said.

Since he had first heard of the case of Philip Toles, he had been wondering how to use this information. How to gain some benefit from a situation he wasn't directly involved in. Now that the sentence had been read and the outrage was beginning, inspired by the statements made by Mr. Corbray and others who believed they had a right to be upset by the judge's ruling, Jabari knew exactly what it was he had to say to Bruna. He only hoped Bruna would be open to the idea, and that she would run it up the ladder to the big boss. The hardcase Jabari knew that people had nicknamed 'The Beast in the Night'. He was only glad he didn't have to deal with that person directly, because Big Bruna was bad enough.

Jabari was aware he would have to deal with the higherups eventually, because what he really wanted was a promotion. He had been doing this work for two years now – since he was fifteen years of age – and while it paid well and he worked for as safe an employer as any in his field, he was tired of days like this. Waiting for rude, crude and hasty clients, waiting for time to move faster. No, he wanted more. And Mrs. Jeffreys' situation was going to help him get it.

Three distinct knocks on the door. His next client.

Jabari was jolted from his thoughts and from the news report playing in his ear. It was rare for him to lose track of time here. The news had completely thrown him off, and somehow an hour had melted away.

He removed the remaining ear bud, the sound of more discussion and examination about the case trailing further from his ear as he put the iPod in the drawer of the desk, forgetting to power it down in his haste.

Jabari turned, looked at himself in the mirror on the dresser opposite the desk. He put on a coat of lip gloss. Smiled into the mirror. Tried to look happy, sexy. Young.

The way they liked him.

"Come in," he said, trying to sound cute and inviting.

The door opened. In came a guy who looked like the last guy, who looked like most of the guys who came to places like this: middle-aged, out of shape, sweaty, eager. He looked Jabari up and down with greedy eyes as Jabari sat on the bed.

"Chocolate," the middle-aged man said breathily, licking his lips as he leered at Jabari's mostly naked skin. The seventeen-year-old was on the bed in a pair of white underpants and nothing else. His current client said,

"How you doing, sugar?"

Jabari hated pet names. Like baby, like honey, like cookie. Like sugar. Especially from strangers. But this was how these men liked to talk. And Jabari knew what they all liked to hear.

"I'm doing fine, daddy," he said, elevating the pitch of his voice. Younger. Always had to seem younger. Which was why he was hairless from his nose to his toes. Which was why he ate so little. And why he wanted a promotion.

Shaving, waxing, and starving himself would only help so much. He was getting older. *Appearing* older. He saw it in the way Bruna sometimes looked at him. Checking him over like a piece of produce nearing expiration. Before long, it would be hard for him to be as young as they wanted him to be.

Information, he thought, letting his mind go back to the case of Mrs. Jeffreys. Soon, hopefully, he wouldn't have to worry about looking so young. But not soon enough.

In his mind, he reminded himself he had three hours left to go. Just three hours. Then he lay down on the bed as the middle-aged man approached him, hands first, mouth open.

FIVE days after Kathleen Jeffreys' sentence was read out loud in court, Mr. Corbray found himself sitting in a place he had hated since his days as a troubled youth.

He was in the principal's office. And he and Mr. Samuels, the principal of Rosenthal P. Straily Public School, had just begun a very uncomfortable conversation.

"Don't tell me you're blaming me too, Morris. I thought we were on the same side here," James Samuels said. He sounded desperate and looked worse. It was the middle of the day, and his tie was already loosened, the Half Windsor knot nearly to his sternum. His jacket was off, draped on the chair behind him. Mr. Corbray could see that Principal Samuels' armpits had drenched his shirt with so much sweat it was threatening to soak the material down to his belt. His face, usually smooth, was days unshaven. His brown hair, since Philip Toles' body had been found over a year prior, had become salted with whites, peppered with greys, and was dishevelled, as it always seemed to be these days.

"We're on the same side, Jim. You know we are. It's not like I'm turning on you. I'm simply taking an opportunity that I can't turn down. No matter what school I work at, no matter what part of the city, I'm still going to defend your name and this school. You know that."

James (Jim or Jimmy to most of the people who knew him personally) grunted, huffed, exhaled. Mr. Corbray was certain the man was physically deflating right there in front of him. Jim picked up the coffee mug full of brown liquid that wasn't quite coffee, brought it to his mouth. Swallowed deep. When he put the mug back on the table, Mr. Corbray caught a whiff of the dark rum inside of it.

The drinking, the man's appearance, these were just a couple of the reasons why Mr. Corbray understood it was time to go. He may not have been turning on Mr. Samuels, who had been under immense scrutiny and pressure from the media, parents, and the school board, but he was certainly abandoning ship. Leaving this man who had worked alongside him in some capacity for the last two decades to drown on his own, provided he couldn't figure out how to stop himself and the school from sinking.

Mr. Corbray had contemplated this moment for quite some time. Even before he had received a call from an old acquaintance of his from teacher's college regarding a guidance counsellor position at a high school in another part of town, Mr. Corbray had been considering updating his resume and sending a few copies out to schools around the city. Though he quickly realized, after the statement he had given following Mrs. Jeffreys' sentencing, that updating a resume might not be necessary. Educators around the country were reaching out to him with offers. He had decided to accept one presented to him by a person he knew and trusted. A person he shared similar interests with. And it was a job that wouldn't require him to move too far away from his ex-wife and daughter, the latter of whom he already didn't see as often as he would have liked to.

It would be more money, but a larger workload; more troubled kids whose lives Mr. Corbray would do his best to change. And less having to deal with the fallout of Philip Toles' death.

He had explained all of this to Principal Samuels, and he was hoping that the man wouldn't make this more difficult than it already was.

"Alright. Congratulations, I guess." Then a pause and another drink from his mug as Principal Samuels looked out the window at a snowy early November day. Searching for something. Not out in the world, but in his mind. Eventually, he must have found what he'd been searching for, or became content with the idea that it might never be found. Either way, something in his face softened and Mr. Corbray could see his old friend in those eyes again.

"Congratulations, Morris. I mean it. No one has had to work this situation harder than you have. You deserve it. Do we at least have you until the end of the year?"

"Thanks for understanding, Jim. Remember, I'm *still* your friend, and I *still* have your back. And yes, I'll be here until the end of the school year. You'll be seeing my ugly mug around these halls for the next seven months."

SIX minutes remaining until lights out, Kathleen Jeffreys noted as she looked at the strapless watch she was allowed to keep in her cell. She had to finish quickly.

The watch was one of a number of belongings sitting on top of what she liked to think of as her desk – a stainless steel shelf that jutted out two feet from the wall it was fused to. Beneath it was a stainless steel stool which was attached to the ground, not unlike the stainless steel sink and toilet combo not far from it. Immediately behind her, across the room, two feet away, was a bed. To her right were bars. To her left, a white cement wall, scratched and graffitied over the years.

For the last seven months, her life had been this six-by-eight-foot cell. She needed out. Desperately.

Now, she finally thought she had a way to do it. To perhaps get her sentence shortened. In her wildest fantasies (which seemed to occur more frequently the longer she was in this facility) she imagined that the judge would be so happy with her and what she had to say that she would be granted permission to leave the prison immediately. To go on house arrest. Or to go free completely.

Because she had information.

She thought it could be important information, but she couldn't get anyone in the prison to listen to her. Even her lawyers weren't taking her calls. The last time she had spoken to a member of her legal team, weeks ago, he had reminded her that they had gotten her an amazing plea bargain, which she should be grateful for. Reminded her that, if she wanted to see her baby again, she had better do the time she had been given. And do it in a well-behaved sort of way. But she couldn't stand another day in this place. It was absolutely terrible.

She had initially been relieved to hear she would 'only' get three years in prison. However, it hadn't taken much time at all for her to understand that three years could feel like three centuries in a place like this. It might have been okay if she had been a bank robber or maybe even a murderer, but prison is particularly unkind to known sex offenders. Especially when those sexual offenses result in the death of a child, and the creation of another which would invariably be chewed up by the foster system. Additionally, Kathleen was a mother who had abandoned two daughters; a deadbeat mom who now had to live among and coexist with many angry, incarcerated women, some of whom had been abandoned or let down by their own parents.

The prisoners all knew her story. And they didn't like her very much. Not very much at all.

It had been over seven months since the sentencing. Each of those months had shown her a new level of sadness and desperation she hadn't known was humanly possible. Never in her life had she thought she would end up in a place like this. She tried to tell herself that it was worth it to have known and loved Philip, but even that was getting harder to believe as each day passed. Especially because she missed her baby so much. Both of them. Philip and their child.

The birth of a baby is, in most cases, a beautiful moment. A monumental occasion. The birth of the child of Kathleen Jeffreys and Philip Toles had been monumental, yes, but there had been no beauty in the event. There was happiness, briefly, before the sadness of the situation had returned to usher happiness out of the room. Along with happiness had gone her baby, taken from her by a nurse. One who was taking orders from a police officer who was taking orders from a judge who was the voice of the people. The front line of society – the societal chain of demand – was in full force in an effort to keep this newborn away from a mother who had been deemed incompatible with that title even before she had given birth. Once a teacher, an educator, a wife, mother, moulder of young minds, now no one thought of her as any of those things. Titles she was compatible with these days were:

Rapist, along with child killer.

Pedophile, also predator.

Unfit, in addition to so many other hateful terms.

Though none of these terms, no matter how vile the insult was, hurt more than that label of unfit. She was already unfit to be a wife. Her husband had divorced her. Made it so that even while one judge was signing documents to have her imprisoned for three years, another had been signing documents to finalize the end of her decade-long marriage. The latter judge also decreed that, for the foreseeable future, Kathleen would have to sever any ties she had to her two daughters from that marriage.

Unfit. For them.

Unfit. For the baby who had still been crying for her as it was quickly removed from the hospital room.

Unfit to teach or ever be around children again.

She had been 'mom' to her daughters, 'Mrs. Jeffreys' to her students. Now she was simply an inmate. A numbered prisoner. That was what society deemed her most fit to be.

This is what Kathleen thought of most throughout her days in lockup. How unfit she was, how much her standing in society had shifted. But mostly what she thought of was her baby being taken away from her before they'd had a chance to bond. She was recalling the memory of that day now as she sat at the metal shelf of a desk inside of her cell. It was torture via remembrance.

She often thought of that memory, and of people, a handful of them. Her now ex-husband was rarely among those people, though she sometimes thought of her daughters and wondered what their lives were like without her. Then she recalled that their lives would be the same as she had intended them to be. If she had run off with Philip as she had been planning to, her daughters would have grown up without her regardless. With the dawning of that simple realization, and as the days had gone by, she found herself thinking of the two girls less and less.

She thought of Philip, of course. Thoughts of Philip were tethered to those of her baby. Thoughts of him in a grave. Thoughts of their baby being just another lost child in the foster system.

There were few happy thoughts.

All of her good memories with Philip were now tainted by what she considered to be society's misguided and hateful judgements of what had been a joyous love. Nurturing care.

Despite so few happy thoughts, she now realized there was one notion that gave her hope. That bit of hope was attached to a man, one of the handful of people she often thought of while behind these bars. Her hope was affixed to information she might have – that she was *certain* she had – on that man.

At first, she had only thought of him because she felt he had betrayed her with all of the mean things he had been saying in court and all over the news. Condemning her. But now she thought of him as a possible way to get out of jail. Thought of him as the real criminal in this situation.

The person truly responsible for the death of Philip Toles.

It was odd that a hopeful, potentially happy thought could be related to a man she absolutely loathed, but it was the loathing of him which made the thought a hopeful one. Otherwise it would simply be one person wishing for the downfall of another. It was the hate she felt for him that would make his downfall a personal triumph for her. One of the few triumphs she could fathom having in a life she considered already over, despite her pumping heart and functioning lungs.

What was life without Philip? Without her baby? It was nothing, nothing at all. But she could make it something if she could be released from here and somehow get their child back. She could feel like she was living again if she could breathe fresh air for more than a few hours each week, if she weren't confined alone in a cage, if she didn't have to live in fear every time she was in the lunchroom or in the yard around the other inmates. Her fellow prisoners seemed to hate her as much as she hated the man who was presently providing her with hope.

She could be free, both mentally and physically, if she could stop being made to feel as though she had done something wrong or immoral. Love, she told herself, was why she was here. And despite hatred helping her to find some hope in this hopeless place, her optimistic epiphany had been aided by love as well.

FELIX I.D. DIMARO

Her love of Philip had made it so she had never stopped trying to figure out his death. She had never, and would never, believe that he had killed himself.

They'd been together the day before he had been found dead. Philip had come to her classroom minutes after she had dismissed her students for the afternoon. It had been home time for most of them, but apparently not for Philip. He'd let her know that he'd had to meet someone at five o'clock that evening. Before that meeting, he needed to kill some time. They had killed the time between Philip's arrival and his meeting with the door to her classroom locked, and all windows covered over. Just the two of them, the world excluded, exactly the way she felt it was meant to be.

He hadn't given her very many details about who he had been going to meet and why, which had caused her concern. But he had assured her that everything was fine. That their plan was still on. He had promised they would run off after school the next day. On his birthday. After he got his classroom cake and got to say goodbye to the few kids he considered to be his close friends.

She knew he had been desperate to get away from his mother. A woman who, Philip had said, spent all of her time drinking wine and chatting to strangers online. The woman barely spoke to her child, criticized him far too often when she did speak to him, and, according to Philip, had once drunkenly told the boy that he was an anchor around her neck. Had told him that she hated cancer. Not because it had taken Philip's father, but because it had taken her freedom. She had told the boy that she would have divorced his father if he hadn't died. And then she wouldn't have been stuck in this shitty city living this shitty life. Mrs. Jeffreys had been set to rescue Philip from that abuse. She knew the boy deserved to be cared for and nurtured, and she had planned to do that for him.

36

The Corruption of Philip Toles

He had been excited. Had told Kathleen that running away with her would be the best gift he could ever receive. That turned out to be the last thing he would ever say to her. He had said those words, then he had smiled at her in that special way that she adored before leaving her classroom to meet the person he was meant to meet. Some friend. An older guy from the neighbourhood she wouldn't have known so his name wasn't important. A guy who he had to talk to before he could up and leave town forever.

Just some older friend.

It took her far too long to figure it out. This was one of her great regrets. By the time she realized who that 'older friend' was and approached her lawyer, her guards, anyone who would listen to her about it, she had already changed and tweaked and smudged her story so often since Philip's death that no one would take her seriously. At first, she'd had trouble believing her theory herself. Had found it nearly preposterous when she had initially said it out loud. And if she hadn't felt preposterous when she had been hypothesizing while alone, she was certainly made to feel so when she was laughed off the phone by one of her lawyers after sharing her piece of information with him.

The guidance counsellor?

Morris Corbray?

Responsible for the boy's death?

Impossible. Especially considering the note in Philip's writing with her name on it. Also, the noose around his neck.

Kathleen had been thoroughly dismissed. As a loon, a conspiracist. A woman desperate to make herself the victim and not the villain.

She persisted with her theory until the lawyer, frustrated by that point, had put his thoughts to her plainly. Said that no one had killed Philip. The boy had hung himself. He'd had a note with her name on it. Had received hundreds of emails from a woman in her mid-thirties telling him how much she loved him and how she was going to take him away from his school, his family, his friends, his life. It was too much pressure for a kid, and he hadn't known how to say no. So, he'd killed himself instead.

"Just focus on serving your time and thinking about how you'll contribute to society when you're released," was the way the lawyer had ended that phone call with her, hanging up before giving her a chance to respond.

That conversation had destroyed her. Had left her feeling as though she were utterly and completely alone in seeing what was such an obvious truth. A truth she didn't think anyone would believe. Until she thought of someone she had been trying not to think of since the day her sentence had been read aloud in the courtroom.

She knew it was an act of desperation to reach out to this person, but by now she was beyond desperate. She needed out, and she needed Philip's killer brought to justice. She could only think of one person who might believe that there was a killer at all. That the boy hadn't killed himself. And that was Philip's grandfather, Solomon Toles.

She didn't know much about the man, other than what she had seen of him in the courtroom and what Philip had told her. But, if Philip was to have been believed, Solomon Toles was just about the greatest grandfather on earth, and the closest thing the child had had to a father after his dad died of testicular cancer when Philip was little more than a toddler. The most difficult part of convincing Philip to run off with her had been overcoming his refusal to abandon his grandfather.

When Kathleen had told him that he wouldn't be able to stay in touch with his grandfather after they ran away, the boy had seemed hesitant. Despite still agreeing to go, and saying he understood that contact with anyone could jeopardize their plans, he had seemed like he might decide to stay with his horrid mother and not leave to start a wonderful life with Kathleen. Finally, she had made a compromise with him. He would be able to contact his grandfather over the phone on certain occasions when they were on the road, but he wouldn't be able to see the man or tell him where the two were staying until Philip came of age and Kathleen couldn't be arrested for being with him.

The boy had understood, and agreed, but told her that he hated the idea of hurting his grandfather even temporarily, although he knew he would have to. He'd said he hated the idea of hurting the feelings of the man who had been his father figure. A man who would do anything for his grandson. Based on Solomon's reaction in the courtroom during her sentencing, she believed that to be so.

Kathleen now hoped he might do – or at least consider listening to – what it would take to bring the killer of his grandson to justice. And to wipe the stigma of suicide from the name and memory of a boy who had been so full of life. Life that an adult he had trusted managed to snuff out, Kathleen thought grimly. Most would have said that the life-snuffing adult was her, but she gave that no consideration. She couldn't think of that. Couldn't think of her role in Philip's demise. Didn't believe she had played such a role. Kathleen saw herself as his hero. Or she would have been his hero if not for that smarmy bastard of a guidance counsellor.

She could think only of blame. Only of getting even with Mr. Corbray. Of her release from this hellhole. She felt as though Solomon would be her final chance, and had set about convincing herself that it was a chance worth taking.

Which was why she was currently rushing to finish the letter she was writing him with the few remaining minutes of light before the prison shut down for the night. A letter begging him to come to the prison and speak to her in person. A letter explaining that there was more to the story than had been exposed in the courtroom. In the media. Because, as she had been left to her thoughts over these last many months, she had gotten to thinking of things she hadn't thoroughly thought of before.

She now recalled the bruises she would find on his body when she was able to see him undressed. Bruises that, when asked about them, Philip had claimed were "nothing". Just some rough play with an older friend of his. That elusive older friend. If only she had pressed him further.

There was also the fact that, on that fateful day, Philip had gone to see Mr. Corbray, but hadn't been able to find him before coming to see her and wanting to kill some time. She now thought back to the constant appointments between Philip and his counsellor. He saw Mr. Corbray every week, sometimes more than once. Mr. Corbray, a single middle-aged man who hadn't shown any evidence of dating anyone or having much of a social life since his divorce a few years earlier. An older man who might have been able to confuse Philip and take advantage of him. A trusted confidant whom Philip might have told about wanting to run off with her, and who might not have wanted that to happen.

Yes, it all made perfect sense to her now. All those mean, mean things Mr. Corbray had said about her in order to remove the guilt from himself. *Of course* he was a child killer. Kathleen was certain of this.

She ignored the fact that she had previously been certain that it was Jim Samuels, the principal, who had killed Philip. Kathleen had also theorized about Mrs. Danielson, the gym teacher who had found his body. These theories were all in addition to her previous notion about Philip's own mother wanting to rid herself of a boy she had never fully committed to taking care of in the first place.

She realized now that those ideas, those earlier theories and suspicions about the others, had been off base, wild, and perhaps stemmed from desperation. But this time she was right. She was certain of it. One hundred percent. She needed to make everyone else certain of it, too. To somehow give the authorities the information that would get her out of this place and clear her name while showing the world the truth.

Someone had to stop that monster, Morris Corbray. Just last week she had seen him in the newspaper. The star guidance counsellor now moving on after slandering her and helping to get her jailed. He was improving his station in life, leaving R.P. Straily P.S. after nearly two decades and taking a job as counsellor at North Hill Collegiate Institute, a high school in east Saturn. She'd pictured a rat leaving a sinking ship when she had seen the news article with its accompanying photo of Mr. Corbray's smug little face. Then, after picturing him as a rat, she couldn't stop picturing what vile things he might be capable of. That's truly when the pieces had started to come together.

She only hoped Solomon Toles would see the truth the way she so clearly could.

She felt almost positive, optimistic, as she quickly scanned over her letter to Philip's grandfather and folded it. Put it in an envelope. Then she put that envelope between the pages of a book, Stephen King's *IT,* a favourite of hers since she'd first read it back in college. She planned for the letter to remain within those pages until the prison staff collected letters to be mailed out in three days. On Monday. In the meantime, she had to keep what she had written safe and away from the wrong eyes. Corbray had already gotten away with too much for too long.

She hoped the staff wouldn't look too closely at the address written on the envelope when she turned it over to be mailed. She wasn't supposed to contact any of Philip's few remaining family members, so she had addressed it to Mr. Toles' business, a small locksmith company in Alberta he ran mostly out of a van, but which he had a PO box for. Kathleen had begged her sister to provide her with that PO Box address.

Her sister was one of the few people who still spoke to her at all, although barely and begrudgingly. It had taken a great deal of pleading and crying, but Kathleen's sister had come through with the information she had needed, and now she would be able to contact the one person who could improve her current circumstances. The only person who could get her out of here and help her get Philip the justice he deserved.

She had convinced herself that Solomon Toles would listen because it was about Philip, and about proving he hadn't killed himself. That had to make him at least somewhat curious. Or so she hoped. It was the first time she had allowed herself to hope since Philip had died nearly two years prior.

One minute until lights out, her watch informed her.

After tucking the book containing the letter safely away among her other books, which were stacked on another metal shelf in the corner of her cell, Kathleen Jeffreys was in bed just as lights out was called and darkness descended upon the prison.

Even amidst the usual cries and screams and crude jokes released into the atmosphere by inmates who didn't know what else to do but that, she was able to go to bed with a small smile on her face, excited for her letter to be sent off in three days.

Hope. It was a lovely thing.

The Corruption of Philip Toles

****

Two days after she had fallen asleep with a small smile upon her face, on a warm and sunny Sunday in June, Kathleen Jeffreys was found dead. Slain. In the prison yard. Someone had punctured her neck with a crude instrument. Repeatedly. Creating holes that allowed her life to leak entirely out of her. A shiv had done it. A toothbrush sharpened to a killing point.

When detained, the person whose hand had held the murder weapon claimed they simply felt as though they'd had no choice but to murder Kathleen Jeffreys.

SEVEN days prior to the murder of Kathleen Jeffreys, a week before the body of the former Mrs. Jeffreys was left leaking in a prison yard with several puncture wounds to the neck, Morris Corbray found himself finally walking away, for good, from the school building he had worked in for the last twenty years. This was seven months after announcing to Principal James Samuels that he had accepted a position at North Hill Collegiate Institute.

It was a fine mid June afternoon. The rare Tuesday that felt like a Friday because it was the last day of school. It seemed to be neither spring nor summer but somehow the best of both. There was soon to be a changing of seasons, not only in terms of weather, but in Mr. Corbray's life and career.

The day had been a special one. Bittersweet. His students and coworkers had spoiled him from the beginning to the end of it. He already missed the school and the people within it as he made his way through the mostly empty parking lot toward his car, but he was glad the day was over. Glad this chapter of his life was over. He was looking forward to putting all the emotions behind him. Not only of the last day, but of the last couple of years since the death that had rocked the school so tremendously. It had been a wild adventure here, perhaps too wild, and it was time to move on. Though, for a little while earlier on, he'd been worried he would never be allowed to do so with the parade of people who had lingered by his office after school to say their goodbyes.

There had been tears, hugs, inside jokes, and promises to stay in touch forever. Promises he knew would be broken, yet which still meant a great deal to him because they were made with the purest of intentions. When a few of his now-former coworkers cried, resulting in him crying, he'd had to remind them all that they would be seeing each other at his official send off party in four days. This coming Saturday, nearly every member of the faculty of Rosenthal P. Straily Public School would gather in his honour at a restaurant in neighbouring Toronto.

Still, impending goodbye dinner or not, it was the end of an era, they had said. And he agreed. But he was looking forward to new challenges. New kids. A bit older than he was accustomed to, but still needing to be guided and shaped into young adults.

Although he was looking forward to future challenges, his present challenge was proving to be more difficult than he had originally thought it would be. He was currently regretting his decision to carry his box of office supplies and the several gift bags he had received that day to his car all in one trip. He was struggling to balance everything in his arms as he tried to fish into his pocket for his keys.

"Need a hand?" a voice said from behind him. A young voice. One he recognized, but vaguely. A student's voice, most likely. Turning around, he was surprised when he saw which student it was. Surprised because he was expecting a current student. Not a former one. One of his favourites. One of his firsts.

"Jabari? Jabari Henry?" Mr. Corbray said. He smiled but was uncertain. Last he had heard, Jabari had dropped out of high school and was leading a questionable life. But here he was, offering to help Mr. Corbray with his things. For no apparent reason. With all the local fame Mr. Corbray had achieved since Philip's death nearly two years ago, he couldn't help but be a bit suspicious of nearly everyone's intentions.

"Yeah, Mr. Corbray, it's me. Can I help you with that?"

Mr. Corbray looked him up and down, then down and up before looking the boy in the face. He was dressed well, wearing a fresh-looking white polo shirt, blue jeans with a belt that was actually cinched at the waist (which wasn't the case with the trousers most boys his age wore these days), and white shoes that were still white. If he were living a questionable life, it seemed to be doing well for him. The boy looked great. Older than Mr. Corbray remembered, but it had been nearly half a decade since he had seen him. That had been after Jabari's eighth grade graduation. Before he went off to high school. It was great to see him now, and Mr. Corbray was glad Jabari looked as though he was doing well, but he was still suspicious. He didn't want to hand his belongings over to his former student.

"I've got it," Mr. Corbray said, then immediately proceeded to drop one of his gift bags. Jabari scooped it up before he could protest, allowing him to reach into his pocket for his keys and unlock the car. He unloaded his burden in the backseat, using the rear driver's side door. Jabari handed him the errant gift bag. He added it to the rest and closed the door.

"Thank you, Jabari. What's brought you back here? Came to say hi to some old teachers? A friend?" He squinted at the teenager, the sun shining in his eyes as he waited nervously to hear what Jabari might ask of him. What he might want.

"Actually, I'm here to see you, Mr. Corbray. I was kind of waiting here, and not for the first time. I've been wanting to talk to you for a little while now but couldn't work up the nerve. And now it's the last day so..." he shrugged.

"You've waited for me here before?" Mr. Corbray asked, looking around him to see who might be watching. The parking lot was practically empty. He had been one of the last to leave the building. "I have to tell you, that's a bit unsettling, Jabari. Especially because you know you can always approach me and talk to me. You don't have to lurk around my car. What's on your mind?" Mr. Corbray was afraid to know, but he had to be nonchalant. Hoped this wouldn't turn ugly somehow.

"That's the thing. I do want to talk to you, but I don't know how to ask you... You know?"

"No, Jabari, I don't."

"I'm trying to figure out how to talk to you the way we used to back in your office. Back when we were alone."

Then Jabari smiled. It seemed to make the boy's face look younger. The way Mr. Corbray remembered. He was suddenly reminded of how much he liked this boy.

"Okay," he said to Jabari. "We can talk the way we used to. Right now, if you want... Do you need a ride?"

PART TWO

RETIREMENT PLANS

ONE month after the beginning of his official retirement, Morris Corbray was treating himself to an evening of celebration. Despite being retired, he was looking forward to the most important promotion of his life.

It was a Thursday night, the first day of October. Nearly thirteen years exactly since the death of Philip Toles. Corbray didn't have the boy on his mind this evening, though. At least not at this exact moment. He still did think of Philip on occasion, but after having experienced so much since meeting the child, he did his best to put Philip and that time of his life behind him. Currently, he was attempting to come to terms with putting his teaching career and working life behind him. The previous month had been the first September Corbray hadn't worked since he was thirteen years old, before he began delivering newspapers on a bicycle fifty-two years prior to his retirement.

Initially, Corbray hadn't thought he would be able to comfortably make the adjustment. He had believed his retirement from the school board would be the end of any further elevation in his life. That he wouldn't have any new goals to look forward to accomplishing. The idea of that had bothered him a great deal, mainly because he hadn't wanted to retire. He had been forced out of his position after over a decade at North Hill, the high school he had moved on to after his time at Rosenthal P. Straily. There had been budget cuts, and expendable members of the staff had been cut along with the budget. In a world where nearly every teacher was trained to counsel youth in some capacity, and where computers handled much of the guidance of those youths, a sixty-five-year-old guidance counsellor just didn't seem necessary. What was necessary, to Corbray, was that he keep all of his pension benefits, which he had been informed would be cut if he continued to teach beyond the age of sixty-five. He had taken the hint as well as the benefits, had agreed to this earlier-than-expected retirement, and had stepped into this new chapter of his life.

On his final day at North Hill, he received the same fanfare he had gotten when leaving R.P. Straily. And he'd cried this time as he had the last. Though this time, the tears he had shed felt far more like those of a mourner than those of one who was gracefully moving on. He had been pleased that his staff and students had loved him at the high school, but he was mostly sad to no longer have a definite direction. Was sad to consider himself as now classed among the old and useless. Especially since, over the past eleven or so years – since shortly after the day he had run into Jabari Henry waiting for him near his car – Corbray had become a man of some importance. Or at least a man of influence.

Shortly after that day, and before starting the job he had recently been retired from, Corbray had been persuaded into joining a social club, membership of which he believed he could only maintain while continuing his job as an educator and counsellor of young minds.

The Corruption of Philip Toles

It was a very exclusive and important club, and Corbray knew he might now become expendable to this organization in the same way he had become expendable as a counsellor.

This organization had become an integral part of his life, fundamental to the way he viewed himself, to his self-esteem, the connections he made, the few people he befriended. This social club had become all encompassing. With his retirement, his potential removal from it was looming. The idea of no longer being part of this group was far more devastating to him than even the loss of his role as an employed educator.

As realization of this potential upcoming loss had settled upon him the previous year, he had turned to God. Had gotten more involved with his community church, and had quickly understood that the church was now where his future should be focused. It was how his social life would be allowed to continue.

After many fundraisers and personal donations, much ministerial training and putting in of tireless volunteer hours, Corbray had been tasked with taking over the position of another retiree. For health reasons, the Deacon of his church was stepping down from his position as leader of the church's youth group. The enthusiastic and eager Morris Corbray had been the obvious choice to be his replacement. This new role was set to start in two weeks.

A promotion, another new beginning. New challenges to look forward to. The best part? His role with the church would keep him enrolled in his social club. A club which had recently announced that, next week, he and a select few others who had performed well for the organization over the years would be rewarded for their contributions. An advancement in their membership along with a vacation. A reward for helping with growth, recruitment, and revenue. He and a handful of others would be taken on a weeklong all-expenses paid trip to an exotic locale. The prospect of retirement had never before looked so good. And that was worth celebrating.

Which is what he was doing tonight. Celebrating the seven-day celebration to come. He was choosing to do so alone for the time being. But that wouldn't be the case all evening.

Corbray was currently at his favourite local eatery. A place recommended to him by his social club years ago, after he had proven to them his worth.

It was a charming place. Part pub, part diner, and entirely welcoming. More importantly, this establishment had a commitment to the community. The restaurant was one of a chain across North America owned by an organization called Helping Hand. Part of their mandate, through this restaurant and other companies of theirs, was to ensure that children who were part of foster systems throughout the continent were given a fair shot at employment. Kids who previously may not have had a chance at a future, or who may have been forced to turn to the streets, were now gainfully employed working in this restaurant's kitchen, as its waitstaff and hosts, and often doing other offsite work for the owners of the establishment.

The place was called Foster's Family Restaurant. Its slogan was 'Where Every Meal Tastes Like Home'. It certainly felt like home to Morris Corbray. It had for over ten years now.

He was in his favourite booth, having been led there by a teenage girl with light brown skin, bright green hair, and more ear piercings than should have been physically possible.

After seating him, the green haired hostess was replaced by a lanky waitress who was in her early twenties, bordering on pale, with flat brown hair and a face that looked like the definition of boredom. She brought to the table the lemon water Corbray had requested of the hostess. He was worried this waitress might turn out to be rude, but she attempted a smile and asked for his order enthusiastically enough.

He smiled back at the bored looking young woman as he pointed to the menu and ordered one of the handful of items he knew they never had.

"Oh. I'm sorry, sir. We don't actually have that available. Someone else ordered it last week and it turned into this whole big deal. I've asked management to take it off the menu but things like that take time, I guess." Now the young lady's face showed some concern. She was likely dreading being admonished for the menu showing an item that the kitchen couldn't supply. Probably wondering why on earth anyone would order pickled beef heart anyway.

"Did the person who ordered the beef heart last week ask to speak to your manager?"

"No. He kinda just yelled a bit until he decided on something else. Are you going to yell at me?"

Mr. Corbray had to laugh at that. The kid no longer looked bored at all.

"Not whatsoever. Don't you worry. But I would like to speak to your manager if you wouldn't mind getting him or her."

The young woman looked both further frightened and also relieved as she immediately turned to get the manager.

It wasn't a long wait before a well-tanned man in his thirties came over. He wore all black, like the rest of the staff. And had long brown hair tied back into a ponytail.

"Good evening, Mr. Corbray," the manager said brightly.

"Good evening, Milo. No pickled beef heart again, it seems."

"No, sir. Would you like a substitute?"

"How about steak tartare? To go."

Morris Corbray rarely ever actually ate at Foster's Family Restaurant.

The manager smiled and nodded. Responded by saying, "Sounds wonderful. I'll be right back with your order."

Milo slid him the black check presenter, the wallet-like book which usually held the bill, before turning to put in his order. Corbray opened it, knowing it would be empty inside, knowing he would get the receipt once his request had arrived. By now he knew the price of everything he ordered here by heart. Reaching into his interior breast pocket, he retrieved several bills which he slipped into the waiter's little black book.

Minutes later, Milo the manager returned with a brown paper bag. Mr. Corbray took it with a smile. It was extremely light, weighing next to nothing, though Corbray was certain it would be incredibly satisfying. He thanked the manager heartily and slid over the check presenter. Milo didn't bother to look at the money, or count it, or offer any change. He responded with an enthusiastic "Thank you!" of his own, well aware that Corbray was a generous tipper.

The price of the steak tartare on the menu, as well as an acceptable tip, would have been covered by a fifty-dollar bill. Corbray had left ten times that amount. The standard one-thousand percent markup he usually paid.

"We hope to see you soon!" It was what the waitstaff said any time a customer was leaving Foster's. And it was what Milo said to Corbray as he prepared to leave now.

He and the manager took turns thanking one another once again as he removed himself from the booth and from the restaurant, eager to open what was inside the bag.

Two

minutes had passed since Morris Corbray had exited Foster's Family Restaurant. He had barely gotten into the vehicle before opening the brown paper bag handed to him by Milo the manager, tearing at it as it sat on his lap. It felt like Christmas. It felt like birthdays.

Inside of the bag was a box. A takeout container.

Inside of the takeout container was the receipt he had been expecting. And nothing else.

Morris Corbray rarely ever ate Foster's food at all.

It looked like any standard receipt. Though upon closer inspection, above and below a set of figures, hidden in plain sight from anyone who might not know what to look for, was an address.

From his glovebox he removed an unregistered GPS navigator. One he only used for times like this, when putting in an order at Foster's. One he could readily dispose of without the addresses entered into it ever coming back to haunt him. This thing he enjoyed so much was more complicated these days with advancements in technology, and everything being so easily traced and recorded.

With the address inputted into the device, he drove, following the automated voice's directions to a place where his appetites would truly be satisfied.

****

It was never the same address twice. At least not twice in a row. Of the many times Corbray had been to Foster's Family Restaurant and had placed this order, he had only driven to the same location on two occasions, and those occasions had occurred over a year apart.

Sometimes it was a condo, sometimes a mansion, other times a discreet little cottage an hour east of town. Tonight, it was one in a row of newly built identical looking townhomes on the outskirts of Saturn's west side.

While the location was rarely the same, the process never varied. He parked his car a block from the house he'd been given the address to and proceeded to approach on foot. When he arrived, he knocked on the front door three clear and distinct times.

A few moments later, the door was opened. While the person who opened the door differed at each house, they were typically the same. The strong silent type. Often large. Always dangerous looking. The type who spoke with their eyes and their body language. The sort of person who simply reached out his or her hand and received into that hand the receipt which had been given to Corbray. He had done this thing many times over the years. This was his least favourite part of the process each of those times.

He hated having the cold eyes of whichever sentinel it was that worked the front door look him over, evaluate and judge him. Whether they did so to make sure he truly belonged there, or they judged him for being there at all, he always felt like some specimen under scientific observation when entering and exiting these places.

"Follow me," the large, dangerous looking sentinel said, placing the receipt in her back pocket after looking it over and determining it was valid.

Corbray followed behind the attendant, up the stairs of the modest townhome and toward a room at the end of the hall.

"Here you go. One hour. And please don't make me come back up here to tell you that you're out of time."

He only nodded, never quite knowing what to say to that. She turned and returned to her post while he stood outside of the room, gathering himself before knocking. Three sharp and distinct raps against the door.

This part always made him nervous.

"Come in," came a soft voice from the other side of the door.

Corbray took a deep breath and entered, a small smile on his face, butterflies in his stomach.

"Hey," he said shyly when he saw who was waiting for him in the room.

"Hey," the boy in the room responded, pretending to be equally as shy as Corbray. He wore only his underpants. Was thin, gaunt, and perhaps not as young as Corbray usually preferred them. But he didn't mind using a bit of imagination when things weren't just as he'd hoped. In less than a week he would be on the vacation of a lifetime with all manner of choices to choose from.

This will be fine, he thought to himself as he removed his coat and hung it up on the hook behind the door. Undid his belt, dropped his pants, and approached the teenage boy on the bed.

Yes, this will do just fine for now.

THREE hours after sitting down at Foster's Family Restaurant, where every meal tasted like home, Mr. Corbray was at home, hungry.

He was always hungry after coming home from Foster's. The irony of this wasn't lost upon him. Neither was the necessity of preparing for these post-Foster's cravings.

He went to his fridge and removed the leftovers from the takeout he had ordered the night before. He placed several Styrofoam and aluminum containers partially full of Greek food on his otherwise barren natural marble countertop. He had asked for at least two of every item he'd ordered, receiving enough cutlery for a small family when the food arrived at his home. As always, he had felt slightly embarrassed upon accepting the large bundle of food from the delivery person. It was a bad habit he had developed over the years, this overindulgence on restaurant meals and fast-food. And it was only when he thought of how bad this habit was that he thought of his ex-wife.

He didn't miss his former partner but sometimes he missed her cooking. More than that, he missed the meals they had shared with their daughter, who was the main reason Corbray and his wife had stayed together as long as they had. But once his daughter had become a teenager, old enough to sense that things weren't right with her parents, old enough to handle the truth, he and the former Mrs. Corbray had quickly realized that staying together for the kid would have been more damaging to everyone than helpful to anyone. The divorce had come shortly after they had come to this realization.

Part of his need to move to another school all those years ago had stemmed from his desire to start a new life as a somewhat recently divorced man; one who had become a quasi celebrity from all the attention and praise he had received, not only because of how he had helped so many students during the time after Philip's death, but also due to his strong testimony against his former co-worker, Kathleen Jeffreys.

His marriage had unofficially dissolved long before the incident with Philip and Kathleen, long before Corbray's days of neighbourhood notoriety. It hadn't been a bad union, only a passionless one. His wife, after years of wondering if she was woman enough for him, had begun to realize it might have been the fact that she was woman at all that was the problem. They had divorced two years prior to Philip's death, parting ways amicably albeit awkwardly.

He had already been optimistic about the changes in his life when he had decided to leave the elementary school, though he hadn't realized at all how wonderful his life could be until the day Jabari Henry had re-entered it.

He thought of Jabari on this night as he prepared to eat his leftovers. His companion, a grey Scottish Terrier named Jar Jar (after the character from *Star Wars*, a franchise Corbray loved) patiently followed him around the kitchen, awaiting a scrap or two of his master's meal.

The boy Corbray had spent an hour with in that room after his brief visit to Foster's had reminded him of Jabari and that long ago day. A day when he had thought he would be getting a fresh new start and a clean break from the drama with Philip. Not knowing that it was the drama with Philip that would go on to shape the rest of his life.

Jabari had offered to talk the way they once had. And Mr. Corbray, despite worrying that it could be a trap, had decided that he'd wanted that kind of conversation badly.

Jabari, five years before he had shown up by Corbray's car, while he was still a student, had been Morris Corbray's first. The experience had been a sickening thrill. The guidance counsellor had never been so excited, but also never so scared. He had worried his wife would somehow see it written on his face each night. But, after some time, once it began happening with regularity, the fear had vanished, leaving only the thrill.

Seeing Jabari years later, older but still youthful, had reignited that feeling inside of Corbray. A feeling he'd thought he'd have no chance to feel again for quite a while considering the events swirling around him during those turbulent times.

For four days he and Jabari had relived those long-ago times, with Mr. Corbray meeting the boy in private again, just like they used to. On one occasion he had, against his better judgement, accepted an invite to the teenager's condo (which had also included meeting Jabari's roommate and co-worker). For the most part, they had spent most of their four days in Mr. Corbray's car or at a motel he knew to be discreet. Mr. Corbray's most important rule was that he never bring any of his young friends (which is how he thought of them) to his own property.

At that point in his life, eyes had been everywhere, his neighbours being the watchful and talkative types. It was part of the reason he had moved outside of the city he had lived and taught in for so long partway through his time teaching at North Hill.

The Corruption of Philip Toles

He had moved to the small town of Courtville, not far east of Saturn City. A place where he could do what he pleased on his premises with no nosy neighbours within a kilometre to disturb him. It was a lonely, secluded life on most days now that he was retired, but he more than made up for those lonely days on the nights he had company. A certain type of company. Guests hired to be there, paid for by the hour, dismissed when they were no longer of use. To Corbray, these were the best types of guests.

Those days of sneaking around and risking being caught by the police or by someone's parents were far behind him, over a decade removed. He had Jabari to thank for that. He also had Jabari to thank for his membership in the social club that had changed his life.

The organization called The Fold.

He was a relatively low-ranking member, but with this impending trip he had the opportunity to move upward within the ranks. Because of this, Jabari was never far from his thoughts. His former student often came to mind when Corbray dined at Foster's, which was one of several secret subsidiaries of The Fold.

Now, as he took a messy-looking plate full of moussaka, pork souvlaki, dolmades, and rice from his counter to his microwave, his dog trotting softly behind him, he thought of his former student warmly. He also recalled when thinking of Jabari warmly wasn't something he had been able to do. There had been a time when Corbray's thoughts of Jabari had been far from warm. A period when his thoughts of the boy had been coldblooded.

When those short four days with Jabari over a decade ago had expired, Corbray had initially wanted him dead. And would have killed the boy himself except he knew he couldn't. Couldn't because he'd been far more concerned with preserving his own life...

Mr. Corbray had finished saying goodbye to those at his goodbye dinner an hour prior to returning to his motel by the water in the south of Saturn City. One of many discreet motels at the end of Coal Town Road. A place most people took to calling Hooker Harbour. He'd checked in before heading to the restaurant in downtown Toronto. The restaurant hadn't been fancy, a standard bar and grill. But everything about that night had seemed perfect to him. He'd enjoyed himself, perhaps a bit too much, because at some point he had stopped saying no to the free drinks. Had been the subject of too many toasts, cheers.

His coworkers, they loved him.

As he slowly staggered down the hallway to his room, he had wondered, with a slightly slanted smile on his face, what those coworkers would have thought about his afterparty plans.

This was four days after Jabari had approached him by his vehicle and had all but propositioned him.

With his new job ahead of him, with that Jeffreys woman behind bars and shunned by society, and with the reintroduction of Jabari to his life, these had been the best four days he could remember. And things were about to get better, he believed, as he successfully managed to get the key card to open the door to his motel room on the third try. He had instructed Jabari to be there waiting, awake and ready for him no matter what time he decided to return from his outing. The celebration of him.

"Daddy's home..." Mr. Corbray had whispered into the mostly dark room. Light had washed in from the hallway, and he had to stop himself from shouting out when he saw a figure standing there in the middle of the room, in the small space between the foot of the bed and the dresser. Then the door closed behind him and it was completely dark again, the shape no longer visible.

The Corruption of Philip Toles

"My God, Jabari! Are you trying to give me a heart attack?" he'd asked as his hand fumbled against the wall looking for the light switch. It took him some time to realize that he was groping the wrong wall.

Jabari hadn't answered him.

The surprise the boy had given him, combined with the liquor in his system, had made him slightly irritable.

"I know I told you to be ready, but why in the hell are you just standing there like some ghoul in the dark?"

"Not a ghoul in the dark," said a softly accented voice that reminded Mr. Corbray of the winds of a brewing storm. "But The Beast in the Night."

Mr. Corbray heard it and felt it at the same time, the thing that had cut through the air and buzzed right past him. It slapped against the wall, a foot above where he was groping for the switch. The feeling of it reverberated down to his palm. Suddenly, the light was on. Something had been hurled at the wall to flip the switch even as they stood entirely in the dark.

Mr. Corbray turned from the wall in surprise, his eyes squinting against the sudden glare.

"Jabari? How in the world did you d—"

At first he'd thought it was the invasion of light into his unprepared eyes that had caused him to begin seeing things. Caused him to see things incorrectly. But as he had allowed his eyes to adjust, two things, in addition to his vision, had become very clear.

His first realization: It was not Jabari standing several feet in front of him in the middle of the room.

The second realization: The person standing several feet in front of him in the middle of the room was not someone Mr. Corbray wanted to be alone in any room with.

He turned to run, stretching his hand out for the door, now truly regretting how much he'd had to drink because he felt sluggish. Slowed down. But so too did the world as he wondered without words, with only bright distress blotting his mind, just how much danger he might be in.

There was that sound again, an object parting the air, the lash of a whip. And this time when he felt it, it was no reverberation. Something was tightly wrapped around Mr. Corbray's hand and wrist.

He looked down and was bewildered to see a black and gold floral patterned scarf twisted around his lower arm. Ensnaring him. Stopping him from making his escape was something he might see wrapped around a woman's head or shoulders.

His eyes made their slow way along the length of the fabric toward its owner, not in a rush to meet the eyes which had already caused him to attempt to flee.

He was tugged, not violently though not gently, by his now entangled wrist, closer into the room. He turned fully toward the person holding the other end of the scarf.

Their eyes met.

'Leave the door alone. Don't try that again,' was what this person's eyes said. This person who had, with barely a twitch of their arm, unravelled the scarf from around Mr. Corbray's wrist and returned it to where it had come from. He watched as the scarf dangled by her left side, one end of it just inches above the carpeted floor. He looked up along the hand which held it, along a body which held atop of it a face that looked like beautiful weaponry.

"Who... wh–" He was attempting to stutter out a question, doing his best to ask this person who they were or what they wanted or why they were doing this. But his question was cut off when the person finally spoke.

"Not a sound, Mr. Corbray."

Then all was quiet for moments, for a minute. Maybe more. This stretching silence was a test to see how well Morris Corbray followed instructions.

"You were expecting Jabari?" the woman finally said after a time. Added, "Another night of rape and child corruption to celebrate your new job?"

"Hey! I resent that! Anyone I have been with is of consenting age. I didn't rape anyone!"

"Is that so? I disagree. I disagree very strongly. But I do not like to argue, nor do I like to be mistaken. Why don't we avoid the argument and see if we can get some outside perspective on the matter?"

The statuesque woman with the sand-coloured skin moved her slender sweater-covered arm without warning, reaching to her right, to the dresser beside her and the stack of papers atop it. Mr. Corbray yelped at the motion of her arm. Then silenced himself, focused on maintaining his dignity, forced himself not to piss his pants right there on the spot. Each time she moved, Mr. Corbray struggled not to release his bladder, not wanting that scarf to lash back out and strike him. Though what struck him next was much worse.

What physically struck him, what flew into his chest and face, were several waxy pieces of paper, hurled at him by the right hand of this deadly looking woman who had appeared inside his room with no invitation or explanation.

"Why don't I send these photos to your family? To your friends? How about your former faculty? Or, better yet, your future faculty? Perhaps the police? I suppose we would eventually get the opinion of a judge or jury. Wouldn't you think so? They would be much better at determining what constitutes rape than someone like me,

if I am mistaken as you claim I am. Is that the route you want to go?"

Mr. Corbray looked down at the photos. This time his bladder did release. He barely felt the spreading heat of his urine as he looked down at the destruction of his career, his future. His life.

These were pictures of Jabari.

These were picture of another, younger boy – Jabari's roommate – wearing little, wearing nothing.

These were all, nearly every single one of them, photos of Mr. Corbray. Also wearing little or nothing.

Doing things the majority of society frowned upon.

A noise came from him just then. A noise like a goose surprised into flight, honking in protest as it took wing. It was a sound he had never made before. It was the only sound he made for some time.

Again, the woman in front of him allowed the time to stretch. Piss dripped from the cuffs of his pantlegs to his shoes, to a pool around them, spreading and overtaking some of the photos on the floor.

Mr. Corbray knew it didn't matter that the photos were being damaged. He understood that these weren't the only copies. That there were others. Plenty of them.

He looked down at the photos, knowing clearly, distinctly, that the boy had set him up. Jabari Henry. From the day he had approached Corbray by his car, offering a hand and more, from far before that day, Jabari had likely had a hand in the plotting of all this.

Nearly all of the photos by Mr. Corbray's feet were of himself or Jabari and his roommate. All except for one. One photo that wasn't explicit in any way.

It was a photograph Mr. Corbray had seen hundreds of times before. On seemingly endless news broadcasts, printed in newspapers, plastered all over the internet.

The Corruption of Philip Toles

It was the smiling face of Philip Toles.

And when Mr. Corbray saw it, his head snapped up.

Again, he went to stutter his 'whys' or 'whos' or 'what-do-you-wants', but a response came to him before he could fully process any of the number of questions going through his mind. Very calmly, the woman said,

"You were involved in his death. The boy, Philip Toles. Is this true or false, Mr. Corbray? Your future depends very much on how you answer this. Please do not lie to me."

She couldn't have known. How could she have known? It was impossible, *he thought. Yet he sensed very much that she did know, and that if he did lie it might be the last thing he ever did. Still, to admit to it might leave him just as dead.*

What if she had been hired by someone in the boy's family? What if she was an investigator? Some agent that would take him in. Lock him up. He would get far more than the three years Kathleen Jeffreys had received. And he was well aware of what was done to child molesters in prison.

He looked at her scarf, thought of the fact that she was in his motel room, had already presented him with evidence of multiple felonies relating to sex crimes, pedophilia, pederasty. With the evidence she possessed, and even with only the speculation of the true nature of Philip's death, she already had more than enough to put him away for many, many years.

There wasn't a judge in the province who would show any leniency toward Morris Corbray. Not with what he would be accused of. And especially not after the way he had played the court, the people, and the media during the time between Kathleen's arrest and her imprisonment.

This intruder had Corbray dead to rights. Caught red handed. If she were law enforcement, he would already be in cuffs.

Still struggling to decide what to say, still strongly considering lying, he observed his uninvited guest closely. Scrutinizingly.

She looked like sharpness.

This stranger's stare was shards of green glass; her cheekbones formed prominent points; her eyebrows had been delicately threaded to form severe angles above her eyes; her nose reminded him of the flesh-rending beak of a bird of prey. And her lips were pressed into razor thin lines as she waited to see if the man in front of her would test her with his dishonesty.

He looked from her face down to the only soft thing about her – the scarf which dangled from her fist. He wasn't eager to feel it again. He looked from her scarf to the rest of her. He saw dark hair. He saw dark clothing. Black jeans, a grey form-fitting sweater. Black leather gloves. Black shoes. Mr. Corbray quickly understood that she wasn't dressed appropriately for the heat of the late spring. No, her outfit was far more fitting for murder. His. That thought decided him.

"I killed him. Yes." He swallowed. It was a strange thing to say out loud. It was the first time he had spoken anything close to the truth of it to anyone. Even as he said this truth, it didn't feel quite real. Nothing felt quite real just then. He felt as though he were watching himself from outside of his body. Waiting, with no control, to see what fate lay ahead of him.

"I'm very glad you decided to be honest with me, Mr. Corbray," the woman had said as she slowly wrapped her scarf around her neck and shoulders. "Now we can get to business."

FOUR hours after Morris Corbray had sat down at Foster's Family Restaurant and given his order, he was sitting at home in his study. Jar Jar was asleep in the doggy bed in the corner of the room.

Corbray's meal was now behind him, no leftovers left. The dishes were washed, as was he after a steaming hot shower. He was in his favourite and most comfortable pajamas, bedtime was approaching, and another joyous tomorrow was only hours away. Yet he still couldn't shake the thoughts of the past that had been at the forefront of his mind since finishing with the boy in the room earlier that night.

He was currently sitting at the large mahogany desk in his study. On that desk, atop his leather blotter, was a wine glass, mostly empty. Along with it was a bottle of red wine which was now nearly devoid of the liquid which had filled it. Most of that liquid had found its way inside of Corbray during dinner and as he sat and read while listening to a collection of Disney movie instrumentals. This combination of activities – Foster's, a favourite meal, a shower, wine, reading, music – usually went far toward helping him relax. But tonight he couldn't completely relax because he couldn't concentrate.

He had just read the same paragraph of Bram Stoker's *Dracula* – a book he read nearly every October – for the third consecutive time, absorbing none of it. He was considering putting down the book altogether when his cell phone rang.

He looked at the display and smiled. He didn't believe in coincidences. And, although he had been expecting a call from her sometime soon, he hadn't been expecting it tonight, much as he hadn't been expecting the bombardment of memories which had preceded it.

He waved away the bit of nostalgic haze clouding his mind and cleared his throat, hoping somehow that it would help him sound completely sober to the person on the other line.

"Hello, madame. I've been anticipating this call."

Her name on the screen of his phone had appeared as "E-16" – a combination of her first initial (the only initial of hers he knew), and the number of times he'd had to change her phone number in his device over the years.

The 'E' stood for Elareen, though people referred to her by many names. Most, as she had first informed Corbray, called her The Beast in the Night when she wasn't within earshot.

Now, on the phone, her voice, which always reminded him of a cold zephyr and chilled him just as thoroughly, was delivering a message that was bringing heat to his cheeks and a smile to his face, despite how icy she still sounded.

She had never warmed up to Corbray since their initial meeting over a decade prior. Not even after he had become a reliable recruiter for The Fold. But whether she was warm to him or not, the business she had proposed to Corbray on that long ago night in the motel room had proven to be lucrative for all involved, just as she had said.

The Corruption of Philip Toles

As he listened to her now, he knew that the path she had led him toward all those years ago on what had started as a nightmarish encounter was about to result in his life becoming, for at least one week, a living dream.

Into his phone, Corbray said "Yes." He said, "Of course." He said, "Thank you, sincerely." Then he hung up the phone, laid his head back against the headrest of his desk chair, closed his eyes, and smiled widely and obnoxiously at the ceiling, relishing this piece of good news, this new access to The Fold. His reward for years of recruiting and grooming.

Elareen had given him the final details of the trip he would be taking in a few days, leaving Sunday and returning seven days later. She let him know where he would be picked up, what he should bring, when to expect an itinerary. This was one of those moments in life when he considered pinching himself because things seemed too good to be true. Because he was starting to feel too lucky.

He felt lucky now due to his conversation with Elareen. It was the opposite of how he had felt nearly a dozen years ago at the dingy motel in South Saturn where the two had first spoken. Because, on that night, he had been sure his luck had run out permanently. In that motel room standing across from someone whose nickname he would eventually learn to understand and agree with, he had been certain he was going to die. Had been convinced that The Beast in the Night was going to kill him...

The longer they spoke, the more certain Mr. Corbray became that he had made the correct decision in choosing not to lie to her. Because the longer the two spoke, the more convinced he was that she would undoubtedly have murdered him otherwise. And might still, if he wasn't careful.

After she had told him her name, what she wanted from him, and what she expected of him, he had asked her how she'd known that he had killed Philip Toles. The answer was that she hadn't, but it wasn't hard to come to the conclusion when the situation was looked at in a certain way. A way Jabari had directed her toward looking.

"Given your encounters with Jabari when he was in your care, it wasn't a far reach to assume you had something to do with the Toles boy, directly or indirectly. You weren't free of the situation, that much was clear to me. Then, there was the number of times he was reported to have gone to your office, including on that final day. And your habit of practically sashaying in front of every news media person or microphone so smugly. It was written all over your face that you were prideful of something each time you talked, no matter how many crocodile tears you shed. It was plain to see for anyone who was looking for it. You're not as clever as you think, Mr. Corbray. Fortunately, I only need you to be as clever as I deem necessary. And I think you can handle that."

After a long pause, some huffing, a swallow, he said,

"Yes. Yes, I can." He didn't know what she was asking of him, but he was clever enough to know to agree.

"Does anybody know that you killed him?"

"I don't... uhh... I don't... no. No."

"Mr. Corbray. I don't like to repeat myself, so I will ask you one final time: Does anyone suspect or know that you murdered Philip Toles?"

He didn't have to think about the question for long. There was only one person who had ever said anything negative about him or his reported relationship with Philip as the boy's counsellor, other than protesters who were angry at the school and the board as a whole.

The Corruption of Philip Toles

"His teacher, Kathleen Jeffreys. She accused me once, I think. But I'm not sure. She started ranting at everyone during one of the earlier court proceedings. She was yelling about society judging her. In the middle of it she pointed straight at me and said she knew the truth about me. She knew that I was the one who had corrupted Philip. Scared the devil out of me. I thought the police would haul me out of the court and straight into the cells right then and there. But then she turned to Principal Samuels and said the same thing. Then Mrs. Danielson. Even Philip's mother. She wound up blaming all of society for ruining him. Then, in nearly the same breath, she said she didn't believe he would ever kill himself. She said some bad kids must have gotten him. The woman was obviously unhinged. I'm sure that's what contributed to her minimal sentence. Even if she does say anything about me, she has changed her story so many times she is no longer credible. Anything she says will sound like the ranting of a madwoman." He shrugged his shoulders. Then he looked away as Elareen bore holes into him with her glare.

"Are you telling me that your freedom and your reputation are being staked on the fact that this woman who the boy professed he was in love with likely doesn't know that you were in the picture?"

"If she knew something, she would have said something right away. That was my greatest worry after hanging Philip up there, that he had talked about me to her. But I had the note they found in his pocket on my side, and I had never emailed him like she had because I'm not an idiot. I assume we wouldn't be talking if you thought I was. It would have been my word against hers, and my word would have been more credible. Or at least less refutable, at any rate. Besides, people trust me. Even if she does think or suspect something, she can't prove it. I was careful. The cameras have me leaving the premises well before he could have killed himself. Before he went to visit my office at the end of the day. Believe me, I know where the dead spots are, which cameras don't work. None of them would have seen me when I came back later. That was one of the reasons I chose to leave him in the gym."

"Why was he in your office that afternoon? Might anyone know or question that?"

"If they were going to question it, don't you think they would have already?" he said sharply, then immediately apologized, regretting both the words he had chosen and the tone he had used to deliver them. Elareen only continued to stare, looking as though she was someone who was practicing patience for the first time. Mr. Corbray quickly continued on.

"He told me about her a few weeks before it happened. He swore to me he had never mentioned me to her, just as he hadn't mentioned her to me for so long. And at first that was okay. Risky, but okay. Then, he told me earlier that week that he was leaving me and leaving town with her on his birthday." Mr. Corbray shifted uncomfortably, looked away from Elareen's cold green eyes.

"I gave him an assignment. That's what I usually did when he started to get difficult. He was to write out why he wanted to leave with her and what his life might be like if he stayed. It was a pros and cons sort of thing. He handed in the assignment during our meeting earlier that same week that I... that he died. When I read it, it immediately read to me like a suicide note, or at least a cry for help. And that's when I decided to do it. I knew I couldn't talk him out of leaving. He was in love. Full on, idiot, head-over-heels, almost-teenage love. And she felt the same. He told me that, and I could see it myself. That

76

greedy bitch was nearly floating around the school while she was plotting to take him away.

"He had been loyal to me up until then, but if he went away, if I became a distant memory, who knew what he might have told her? I had to risk it. I couldn't let him leave with her. So, I told him to take a few days, think it over and meet me after school the day before his birthday to see if he still felt the same.

"He was accustomed to walking in and out of my office. He and a few of the other kids with family issues in the school were in and out of there so often no one questioned it. He found a coded note telling him I had an emergency to take care of but that I would meet him later, at a place we sometimes met up. Then, when he showed up, I did what I had to do. I brought him back to the school and... Well, you've read the news articles. They found him hanging. I took the note I had left him asking him to meet me out of his pocket, then I replaced it with the note – the assignment – he had written me. He never put either of our names on anything he wrote to me. I warned him about that for the sake of discretion. But he didn't mind including her in his note to me. We had a really trusting bond that way.

"When the assignment was found in his pocket, it was interpreted the way I expected it to be. As a suicide note. Philip made a typo as he was writing the assignment. In the final line, he had meant to write 'Mrs. Jeffreys made me so many promises. If I don't do this, she'll feel bad about that.' referring to letting down Mrs. Jeffreys if he hadn't left town. But he had accidentally left out the word 'don't', so it read, 'If I do this she'll feel bad about that'.

"The moment I saw the mistake, combined with the lines he had written before it, I automatically thought it looked like he was blaming her. I tore off the rest of the

note, leaving only the part that implicated that whore. I cut away whatever didn't add to the illusion of suicide. After that, I hoped the police would see it as I had intended them to. Which, of course, they did. That woman was rightly put in prison, and we can all move on with our lives now."

There was another stretch of silence. By this point, Mr. Corbray was beginning to understand that this was part of the way Elareen communicated. She let the intimidation seep into the skin, settle into the soul. He felt as though he might shrivel under her scrutiny.

"You have a lot to learn," she said, finally.

"Meaning what?" he asked timidly, terrified this was a threat.

"Meaning that you can never leave anything, especially your livelihood and our potential business arrangement, to chance. There is much to be gained here. It would be a shame to lose it all before we have even started."

"She'll be in prison for three years. And she's doing her time in another part of the province because of how hostile things were for her here. People practically burned down her house, chased her husband and kids away even though I'm certain they were planning on leaving anyway. The point is, no one believes anything she has to say. Trust me. She can rant and rave for the rest of her life and no one will believe her." He thought that if he said this confidently enough, he might be able to talk away the creeping sense of dread he felt climbing up his spine. The sense that he had forgotten something, left something unfinished. Some business unsettled. And here he was being reminded of how crucial that unsettled piece of business was.

"She won't be completing her prison sentence. Of that I am certain," Elareen responded.

"Why?" Mr. Corbray said, almost too harshly. He worked to temper himself before adding, "Because the system is easier on women who do what she did than it is on men? I don't think that will matter at this point. The outrage over the original three-year sentence was bad enough. I don't think she's going to be getting early parole."

Elareen had only stared, letting the silence soak in yet again. With it came realization.

"Oh, you mean... Oh..."

"Nothing to chance, Mr. Corbray."

And that was why, the day following his conversation with The Beast in the Night, a warm and sunny Sunday in June, Kathleen Jeffreys was found dead. Slain. In the prison yard. Someone had punctured her neck with a crude instrument. Repeatedly. Creating holes that allowed her life to leak entirely out of her. A shiv had done it. A toothbrush sharpened to a killing point.

When detained, the person whose hand had held the murder weapon claimed they simply felt as though they'd had no choice but to murder Kathleen Jeffreys...

Over a decade removed from that day, Corbray was continuing with his evening after the brief interruption that was Elareen's phone call. He spared one last thought for Jabari. Other than Philip, Jabari had made the most difference in the trajectory of Corbray's life. He had no idea where the young man was now, hadn't seen him since those torrid four days, and wouldn't dare ask Elareen about the former teenage prostitute's whereabouts.

He had resented Jabari for a long while after that initial meeting with Elareen, but those resentments had faded as his business with The Fold increasingly became more profitable and pleasurable. Now, with the most pleasurable vacation he had ever anticipated only days ahead of him, he wished he could thank his former student. Wished he could thank both Jabari and Philip.

Turning up his music (currently playing was *The Lion King's* 'Circle of Life'), he picked up *Dracula* and flipped to the page he had dogeared prior to answering the phone. Before he tackled the paragraph he had been stuck on for a fourth time, he couldn't help but chuckle. Never would he have thought that two murders would lead him to the life he had always dreamed of.

He continued to have trouble focusing on the novel as he thought of what lay ahead for him. The trip this coming weekend, this step closer to being part of the inner circle of The Fold. He may have just retired but, in this moment, Corbray felt as though his life was only just beginning. He had so much to look forward to.

Bringing the glass of red liquid to his lips, he sipped, he swallowed. He smiled.

PART THREE

NEWSPAPERS

"ONE hell of a trip," was the response Morris Corbray gave his driver from the back seat of a black Lincoln MKS as he was picked up from the airport and asked about his vacation.

He had just returned from perhaps the greatest week of his life. Though, as he was driven first to the kennel to pick up his dog, then to his home, he only talked about the weather, the food, the drinks. Generic things.

Although the driver was provided by The Fold, Corbray knew not to mention anything that had happened on his trip. Non-Disclosure Agreements had been signed, indirect threats had been made. The rest of the world, the driver included, could never be told where he had just been.

New Eden Isle.

To the driver, to Corbray's daughter, to the members of his church, to everyone who mattered, he had just been on a singles cruise for a week. Fake photos had been staged in the event that anyone requested to see them. He had even sent a few to his daughter to add to the pretense. In truth, a singles cruise was the last place on Earth he would want to be, but the cover story had worked well. He had gotten to go to New Eden Isle, and had also received a bit of a reprieve from those who questioned why he was still single so many years after his divorce. The trip had given him a way to say, 'Hey, I'm trying' when his family and friends inquired about his dating life. Even as a divorcee, people became suspicious when a man, especially one who worked with children, lived by himself for too long.

The trip had gone without a hitch, which was an understatement, really. The trip, to Morris Corbray, had been perfect. It had been worth the wait. Worth dealing with the stress of that first encounter with Elareen, and each uncomfortable encounter with those in her organization thereafter. Worth the scrutiny because they had invited him into a piece of paradise.

Corbray was already missing the boat bashes, the nighttime beach parties. All the boys and all the drinks. And no judgement. No fear of being caught and being exposed. In fact, being exposed took on a new and wonderful meaning during his week on the island. Being exposed in that wonderful way only meant one fit in with the rest of the crowd.

Everyone there had been just like him.

It had felt as though Heaven had fallen and landed in a place only he and a select few could access. He smiled as he thought of it. And while he missed it, he understood, with a great deal of satisfaction, that this trip to his personal Heaven would be the first of many. He had only been given access to a small part of the island on this vacation. There was still so much to explore, and further levels for him to rise to within the organization, he reminded himself. Even heavenlier Heavens were in his future.

Life was good. He had a bounce in his step when he got out of the car after arriving at his house. He even declined the driver's offer to help with his belongings, hefting his own luggage from the trunk before grabbing the dog carrier from the back seat. Inside of it was Jar Jar, the Scottish

The Corruption of Philip Toles

Terrier he had considered to be his best friend for the five years Jar Jar had been alive and under Corbray's care. The dog looked out at him with stress in his eyes. He never enjoyed these long rides in the miniature cage.

"We'll be inside, and you'll be out of that thing soon, little guy. Don't you worry," he said, still smiling. Even the dog felt lighter in his carrier. This was the best, strongest, the most limber and spry he had felt in a dozen years. This reminded him, once again, of his forced retirement, and how he wasn't quite ready to call it quits. He felt like he still had so much to give to the youth.

The fact that he didn't have to work a full schedule and could continue to be useful to The Fold was something he considered to be a life saver. Literally. He had always imagined that once he lost his job, Elareen and The Fold would cut him off, or worse, eliminate him in order to maintain his silence. However, when he had broached the topic with Elareen, fearful of what she would say, she had only reminded him that not all clients were contributors. So long as he could pay, he could still play. As relieved as he'd been to hear that, he hadn't wanted to simply be a client. He wanted to be an asset. And now he would continue to be one.

In two days, he would begin his run as the youth leader at the local church. He knew he couldn't be as productive as he'd been as a counsellor at a school with hundreds of students to choose from, but he could still recruit. He was certain of it. He was feeling pretty certain in general, feeling optimistic. He said goodbye to his driver and took in a breath of fresh air on this warm October day.

Yes, life felt perfect just then as he walked to and entered his home, whistling a tune he wouldn't have been able to name if asked. Some sultry song he had heard on vacation several times.

After entering his house and removing his shoes, the first thing he did was release his dog from the carrier. Jar Jar yapped as usual, seeming to be in the same good mood as his owner now that he was out of the little cage. It was likely this elevated mood Mr. Corbray was experiencing, the wide-eyed optimism, that stopped him from seeing what had been left in his foyer for him.

Even when the dog had collected the item and brought it to him, it took him a while to register that there was something wrong about it. Something years out of place. The dog had brought to his owner a newspaper, which was rolled up to form a tube, and held that way by a rubber band. Corbray couldn't remember the last time he had seen a newspaper on his property, let alone in his house. Not since everything had become digitalized and placed on the interweb.

"Where did you find this, Jar Jar?"

The dog, of course, didn't answer. But he didn't need to. As Corbray looked up, he noticed that there was another rolled up newspaper at the base of the steps leading upstairs, several feet away.

"Oh..." was the sound of surprise Corbray made as he saw yet another rolled up paper on the third riser, another on the sixth, on the ninth. There was a rolled up newspaper perched with an end jutting over the edge of the landing at the top of the flight of steps. He was baffled as he looked at the trail of rolled up newspapers leading to the second floor.

Corbray didn't know what to make of it. But Jar Jar apparently found the prospect exciting. The dog began to run back and forth between his stunned and frozen owner and the newspaper rolls, bringing each to him individually before running to get the next. Jar Jar hadn't fetched a paper since he had been a puppy, when newspapers were more commonly found. The dog seemed to be making up for lost time.

Corbray watched Jar Jar, trying to figure out what was going on. His door had been locked while he had been away. His daughter had a key to the house, but there was no reason she would have left bundles of newspapers on his staircase. He wondered if this was some sort of a prank. People broke into houses and did strange things all the time. Prank or otherwise, he had been considering getting a security system for some time. Now he felt that perhaps the time for consideration was over.

Jar Jar brought Corbray the newspaper that had been perched at the top of the landing, then darted back up the stairs, bolting around the corner and out of sight. Corbray was in the process of bending to pick up one of the newspaper bundles now at his feet when he heard the sound of his dog sliding over the hardwood floor, then the sound of the dog crashing into something. Then barking.

His heart thrashing from worry for his best friend, Corbray abandoned the bundles of newspapers by the door and ran to see what had become of Jar Jar.

TWO steps at a time, Corbray flew up the stairs, his body thoughtlessly responding to the panic he felt over the distress of Jar Jar. The dog was barking wildly.

He couldn't recall the last time he'd sprinted up a flight of stairs, and wouldn't have thought he could have dashed up this flight as fast as he was going had he been asked before doing it. But he was moving automatically. If anything happened to his dog he would be absolutely devastated. He didn't want to think about it, but couldn't think of anything else as he hit the top landing.

Once standing on that top landing, he stopped, suddenly with a lot more to think about.

The bathroom was the door immediately in front of the staircase. On either side, at both ends of the hall, were rooms. His study and the guestroom to the left, the master bedroom, where Jar Jar was currently barking loudly, to the right. The master bedroom door was ajar, though not open enough for Corbray to clearly see into the room. He had gotten to the second level of his house intending to turn right and keep on running until he was through that sightly open door, but now, as he looked at the floor, he found himself temporarily unable to move.

More newspapers.

The Corruption of Philip Toles

This time they weren't in rolls. The newsprint had been unrolled, unfolded and lain out – one long grey paper at a time – all over the hardwood floor of the second level of his home, reminding Corbray of the bottom of a bird cage. He felt much like a captive bird at the moment as he wondered who might be looking into his cage at him. Who might be trying to rattle that cage. He wondered who it was that had been in his house. Couldn't help but think that whoever it was might still be inside of it even now.

It was that last thought that prevented him from continuing to head hastily toward his bedroom, the entry to which the trail of newspapers led. Some of these had been strewn about from their careful placement on the floor by Jar Jar's paws as the dog had run into the room.

He was still barking.

"Jar Jar? You okay, boy?" Corbray called out, talking to the dog as though he were a human, the way he always did. Usually, he did this without expecting any answer, though this time he was desperate for some sort of intelligible response from his pet.

He was able to breathe a sigh of relief when the dog gave him a response by emerging through the partially open door of the room, his tail wagging, looking around at the newspapered floor and not quite understanding what game was being played here in the hall with the usually smooth and uncovered surface.

Corbray didn't understand what game was being played either.

The dog ran to him, slid on a paper as he tried to halt in front of his master. He crashed harmlessly into Corbray's shins, yipping excitedly. Looked up at his master, tilted his head as if to ask why the old man wasn't joining in on the fun.

Corbray would usually have bent down to pet his best friend, but he couldn't be bothered with the dog at the moment because he was looking at the papers for the first time. Looking at them not as a collective mass all over his floor, but as papers with information printed on them; pictures, words and sentences forming stories and providing knowledge to the public. As what was printed on the newspapers registered in his mind, he began to hope that this was only a prank. Not something more malicious. More ominous.

Jar Jar gave his owner an impatient yip, then turned and skidded back toward the bedroom, treating the hallway like a Slip 'N Slide. Corbray followed, his eyes glued to the newspapers on the ground.

He saw names. He saw faces.

He recognized them all.

His name was there, his face also. It was younger in these photos, but still easily recognizable. He stepped over his face a time or two as he walked on the papers to the room with the partially open door.

He hesitated to push the door completely open, not only scared that he might find the intruder still in his home, in his room, but that he might discover something worse than what he had already seen on the newspapers he was standing on. Something more direct than what these papers seemed to be saying.

Deep breath.

He pushed open the door.

A step. Across the threshold. A step. Into the room.

Exhale.

When he went to inhale again while observing the room, his breath hitched. It seemed, as he looked around him, that Morris Corbray had forgotten how to breathe.

The Corruption of Philip Toles

The dog had created little piles of newspapers all over the place, sliding into and bunching them up with the force of his body. Against the furniture. Against the walls. But Corbray paid neither Jar Jar nor the papers on the floor any mind, because there were plenty of these same newspapers taped up on the walls. On his mirror. All over. Taking up every inch of space. Showing him those same names, those same faces. Though there was one face which dominated the others, one that was the subject of each and every single one of these many news articles.

Everywhere, all around him, he saw the smiling face of Philip Toles.

T**HREE** photographs of Philip had been widely circulated in the wake of his death, in the frenzy of news media reports, the uproar among the town.

The first and most commonly seen, the one which had been on all of the front pages when Philip's death had been front page news, was the same photo which had been used in his class yearbook the year before he had died.

It was a 'Picture Day' picture, and though it had been printed in black and white, Morris Corbray knew that the shirt Philip wore in the photo was orange with white stripes. He also knew that Philip hadn't liked that photograph very much. The boy had hated to be seen without his ballcap on. But the newspapers had seemed to like the photo, and had run with it. That image of Philip smiling for the professional photographer had been all over town for months.

The second of the photos of the deceased boy had been that of Philip on a fishing trip with his grandfather. In this photo, Philip was wearing a black Fred Flintstone tank top and his favourite red hat. Both he and his grandfather were looking at the camera and presenting modest catches, though, by the look on Philip's face, one would have thought he had reeled in the largest fish ever caught. His smile beamed bright even through the black and white image that Corbray was looking at now. Even through the years.

The third image had been of Philip playing basketball as a member of the school team in the sixth grade, before the seventh grade when Philip's mother had started to truly spiral and he had quit sports as a result, finding less child-friendly extracurricular activities to partake in.

With his teacher. With his counsellor.

The newspapers, which were taped up all over the room that Corbray was currently spinning in, detailed that Philip had changed that year, during the seventh grade when he had fallen into the clutches of his social studies teacher.

What the papers didn't describe was the fact that the guidance counsellor had also taken advantage of Philip. Corbray now believed, as a layer of cold sweat coated him everywhere, that whoever had posted these papers on his walls was trying to make that point very clear.

'Your name is here, Mr. Corbray,' he could imagine the person who had done this saying. 'Your name is here, but not as it should be. It should have been you on trial.'

For rape.

For pederasty.

For murder.

There might have been a million different words in print on the papers pasted up before him, but, to Morris Corbray's eyes, each of them said 'you'. Rearranged and reread, at a second glance, all of those million words said 'guilty'.

He raced to the wall across the doorway. Began to tear at the newspapers, savagely ripping them from the wall while Jar Jar barked excitedly behind him. Yipping, still thinking it was a game. More papers to play with rained down on the dog as his owner seemed to have become, at least partially, a blur. Ripping and throwing, tearing and tossing papers down upon the floor.

A game, to the dog.

A game, Corbray realized, as he was stunned to stillness for the second time in a matter of minutes, was being played with him as well. Because there was something behind the newspapers on the wall he was tearing at. Something scrawled there.

Something painted in black.

Corbray collected himself. Or at least tried to. He counted down from ten. Attempted breathing exercises. Failed. He still hadn't quite remembered how to accurately respire.

He brought his hands back to the wall. Shakily, slowly, he began to tear again, this time not stopping until the entire wall was absent of its makeshift wallpaper. Didn't stop until what was there was clear.

He stood back, watched with shaking hands, moistening eyes, and a thundering heart that seemed to be the drumbeat to his doom. On the wall, spray painted there, he was looking at more words. Two:

HAPPY ANNIVERSARY

FOUR hours after Corbray had uncovered the words **HAPPY ANNIVERSARY** scrawled upon his wall in a childish and awkward font – a font that, to him, looked uncomfortably familiar – he finally sat down and attempted to relax for the first time since coming home from his vacation.

Before he had been able to sit down, he'd made certain his house was empty, had double-checked that each door was locked, then had immediately gone to purchase paint, painting accessories, and large garbage bags.

Now, after putting these items to use, he was in his study, a glass of rye on his desk rather than his customary red wine. He needed something to calm his nerves after an impromptu afternoon of cleaning and painting. He had spent the last several hours collecting the newspapers (much to Jar Jar's chagrin) and hauling what had resulted in five garbage bags full of newsprint to his workshop behind the house. After that, he had repainted his bedroom, a chore he hated even under normal circumstances.

After trying to figure out what to do about the situation, he was sitting at his desk, his music not playing like it typically would be. He chose not to play his Disney instrumentals this evening in order to better allow him to hear the doors, the windows. He had a sudden need to hear every sound made inside his house. Hoped not to hear sounds indicating that someone was trying to come in from outside of it.

The rye wasn't the only item that wouldn't normally be on his desk. Instead of a book, on Corbray's desk in front of him, was a gun. It was a Beretta M9. A nine-millimetre semiautomatic pistol.

He had a decision to make.

The gun was a gift. More accurately, it was an insistence from Elareen. The Beast in the Night had put it in his hand not long after they had agreed upon the terms of their business arrangement. That was the way she had stated it. Business. That was how he liked to think of it.

In truth, it was simply compensated blackmail. He had no choice in the matter. By virtue of what she knew about him, the photos she possessed, the information she had, she owned him. It was much nicer to think of it as a business arrangement than as his perpetual servitude. So, when Elareen had handed him the pistol and said, "If you believe you're at risk of getting caught, use this," Corbray had chosen to take it as friendly, albeit grim, advice from a business partner. Perhaps encouragement to defend himself if things became ugly.

It was easier to believe that than to see the gesture for what it was: a veiled threat. A gift that said, 'If you screw up, and you even think of talking to someone about anything you know, blow your brains out of your skull. Because what will happen if you don't kill yourself will be much, much worse.'

He had a decision to make, but suicide wasn't an option.

Corbray had always believed he could come out ahead in any situation. Had done so throughout his life to this point. Why should that change now? Some kook with a bunch of old newspapers wasn't going to scare him into thinking that a secret nearly thirteen years old might suddenly be unearthed. No, if this person knew something, they would say something, or ask for something. This was just a prank from a local who had found out about Corbray and the old case.

The person had probably gone online and read all about Philip's death, the backlash R.P. Straily and its staff had faced, and had decided to play this little joke on the former educator and counsellor. People were nutty these days. They had a lot of time on their hands and meanness in their hearts. That was the real issue with society, he thought.

The gun in front of him was in case one of those mean-hearted people attempted to break into his home again. The decision he had to make was whether or not to tell Elareen about what was going on.

He had quickly decided that he could not tell the police. That hadn't required much thought at all. It simply wasn't an option. Besides, Elareen could provide him with the security he needed. She could likely find out who had been in his home if she chose to use her influence to do so. But, the thing was, she could also become concerned about him being a problem. A risk. Association with him becoming a chance she wasn't willing to take.

Corbray knew what happened when Elareen didn't want to take any chances. He thought of Kathleen Jeffreys, of her torn open neck. He understood that telling someone whose nickname was The Beast in the Night about a potential problem to her multi-million-dollar organization might not be a wise thing to do.

No police. No Fold.

He only had one option, other than to keep himself armed and ready at all times. And that was to get a security system. He would also have to stay diligent. Keep an eye out for someone who might have an issue with him, someone who might want to play games like this with his life.

His life... He thought of it now as things seemed to truly be in jeopardy for the first time in his adulthood, other than during that initial meeting with Elareen. Even his divorce had been smooth, a blessing in so many ways.

He had much more living to do.

He was starting his new role at the church in a matter of days. New children, new opportunities. He thought of New Eden Isle, thought of all the possible wonders in his future if things did not go off the rails now.

He thought, as he clutched his gun:

I have far too much to live for to let anyone play games with me. And if they keep trying, I'll be ready.

FIVE garbage bags full of newspapers. That's what was on Morris Corbray's mind the moment he woke up on the morning after returning from the greatest vacation he had ever taken. Those five bags among many other things.

The other things on his mind came in the form of questions. Questions such as:

Who had been in his house?

Was there someone who knew his darkest secret and was threatening to bring it to light?

Was someone out to ruin everything he had worked to attain? To deprive him of the marvels he had seen as he advanced up the rankings of The Fold?

Also on his mind was the fact that he had killed before when he'd had far less to lose. Killed when it hadn't been a certainty he had anything to lose at all. He would kill again if it meant hanging on to all he had now. Would do so happily.

Five garbage bags full of newspapers, self-preservation, and murder. That was what was on Corbray's mind the morning after he returned home from his vacation.

He couldn't yet do anything about murdering the person who had given him such a poor night's sleep with yesterday's prank, but he could certainly get rid of those papers, and get one portion of this dark joke out of his mind.

He sat up on the couch in his living room, where he had slept while the paint in his bedroom dried overnight. Removed the thin sheet he had spread over himself. Stretched, rubbed his temples. The whiskey from the night before reminded him that he should perhaps stick to dry red wine, or at least not allow the two to mix as he had throughout the previous night.

He checked the clock on his wall, saw that it was six minutes past eleven. He wasn't used to sleeping in this late, though his night had been more full of tossing and turning than it had been of slumber. He felt as though he hadn't slept at all.

"Jar?" he called out to his dog as he dragged himself through the living room into the attached kitchen which led to his back door. Jar Jar waded over from the hallway entrance, likely just coming down from his usual spot upstairs in the corner of Corbray's office. He was relieved to see Jar Jar. As though he thought the dog had been in danger.

He wanted to deal with the garbage bags in his shed right away, even though his body, his head, all of him wanted to return to his couch or, better yet, to his bedroom to try get some restorative sleep. But he knew he wouldn't be able to sleep with those bags out there. He needed them gone immediately.

It was fall, and people in this area still burned their leaves during the season. He decided he would burn the newspapers along with the bags of leaves that had been in the workshop since the last time he had raked, shortly before his trip.

He put on the beat-up pair of runners he kept near the sliding patio door. Walked out the door with his dog by his side. Was surprised to find how much he enjoyed the fresh air on this unusually warm October morning. Nothing like a breath of nature when you've spent a night feeling as though your life is being threatened.

Just a prank, he reminded himself. *Some idiot kid having fun because he or she heard some rumours about my old job. That's all.* It was one of the many things he had been telling himself since he'd seen the writing on the wall. Something he was struggling to believe.

Jar Jar had immediately abandoned him on his walk to his elaborate shed. The dog had gone from walking by his master's side to running off after a squirrel, chasing it up one of the many trees in the expansive backyard.

Corbray smiled at the scene. Seeing Jar Jar having fun always made him feel better about things. Currently it made him wonder if perhaps he was overreacting to a practical joke as he felt the weight of the pistol he had put into the pocket of his pajama bottoms. The pistol he had kept on the floor within arm's reach of his spot on the couch throughout the night. It was better to be safe than sorry. His life was on the line one way or another.

Quickly cutting across his large back lawn, he reached his shed – the outbuilding he thought of as his workshop. Both the terms workshop and shed weren't appropriate titles for the structure. It was large enough to house two cars, and could comfortably operate as a small guest home if he had any interest in turning it into one. But he didn't. He didn't like guests staying over, and he certainly wouldn't want them to have access to what he stored inside this shed along with his tools, landscaping equipment, bags of leaves, and now the five bags of newspapers.

Corbray unlocked and removed the padlock he kept on the handles of the double doors. He slid the double doors apart. Looked in. And, for the third time in less than twenty-four hours, he was stripped of the ability to move by disbelief. He stood still, looking at the empty space in front of him. Staring at the spot on the floor where he had left the garbage bags the night before. Now, as he scanned around the workshop, he saw that each of them – every one of the five bags full of newspapers – was gone.

****

He searched all over his shed for the bags of newspapers. They were nowhere to be found. As he came to the realization that they were truly gone, he understood that they were not of great importance at the moment. Not compared to what else might have been taken from his shed.

Corbray ran to the far side of the elaborate outbuilding. Past the couch, the desk, the dart board. Past everything that made this place feel like his personal clubhouse. He sped toward one of his work benches. Once he made it to the bench, he pushed it back from where it had been placed until it was against the wall, several feet from where it had originally stood. Beneath the spot where the bench had been, he removed six pieces of tongue and groove planks, each roughly four feet in length and six inches wide. What those planks revealed was a space between the shed floor and the ground underneath it.

In that space was a waterproof hockey bag. It was a faded red, black, and white Chicago Blackhawks bag, his favourite team despite him growing up and living near Toronto, Maple Leafs country.

He was usually happy to see this bag with the head of a smiling cartoon Indian emblazoned on its side because he was always happy to see what was inside of it. Now, though he was relieved to see the bag, he wondered if what should have been inside of it still was. Or if it was gone, vanished along with the newspapers.

His heart raced with such speed and intensity that he was genuinely concerned he might collapse here, die on this spot, his body to be found half in his sacred hiding place. He wondered what his old coworkers, his family, and the media might make of such a grizzly discovery. Especially considering what he had hidden here in this hole. If it was still hidden here at all. It wasn't exactly the sort of legacy anyone wanted to leave behind after they had departed.

He shook the morbid thoughts from his mind and focused on the bag. There was a combination lock on it keeping the double zippers secured together. His fumbling fingers failed to put the correct code in several times before he got it right.

Corbray removed the lock. Unzipped the bag. Looked in.

Relief rushed through his body, filled him, then escaped him quickly in the form of a soft sigh from his nostrils. He released not only air from his lungs but some of the tension in his chest. His heartbeat slowed. He was thankful, which was not something he would have imagined being while in the middle of this strange ordeal. But he was.

He was thankful because his purchased magazines and movies, along with his personal photographs and videos, were still inside the hockey bag. It looked like it was all there: VHS cassettes, physical photos, computer disks and DVDs; several flash drives and an external hard drive as well. His life's work. His greatest collection. While this was a relief, he quickly went back to worrying over the fact that he couldn't find the bags of newspapers.

After covering his sacred hiding place with the planks, and pulling the workbench back over the secret spot, he decided to search around and behind the shed for the bags, hoping he had perhaps absentmindedly put them there by mistake. It was a desperate hope that proved to be short-lived. The bags of newspapers were not behind the shed among his firewood. Nor were they beside the shed near his compost bin.

Abandoning the backyard (and Jar Jar, who was now chasing his tail instead of a squirrel), he went to his garage at the front of the house. This was another desperate hope. Another disappointment. The newspapers were nowhere to be found.

Finally, the most desperate of desperate hopes came with the thought that he may have simply left the bags in his newly painted room, though he didn't think this was likely. He distinctly remembered hauling the bags to the backyard, returning to the house, and then painting over the words that had been sprayed on his bedroom wall. Still, memory could be a funny thing, he convinced himself. Perhaps he was mistaken.

He walked into his house, toward his bedroom, leaving Jar Jar to do what dogs do in backyards. He was glad he'd done so, because loud noises – screams – startled the dog. And the dog would have been mightily startled – just as startled as his master – when Corbray let out a cry of anger and frustration after entering his room.

The bags weren't there, that much was clear. But it wasn't what was not there that troubled him, that had his heart and his mind racing, not knowing how to settle. What troubled him deeply was what *was* there.

On the wall, the same wall Corbray had painted over the previous day, were the same words he had covered with a coat of paint. They were re-scrawled and sprayed more messily, more angrily than before. As though the person responsible was upset that the original had been covered. On the wall, the same message, reinforced:

HAPPY ANNIVERSARY

SIX hours after he had found the words **HAPPY ANNIVERSARY** scrawled on his wall for a second time, Morris Corbray was sitting in his daughter's living room, on the couch, her four-year old son on his lap.

It was approaching six in the evening. His daughter, Sheila, was in the kitchen of her cozy apartment, preparing them a meal. Jar Jar was asleep on the one-seater across from his owner, likely exhausted from being driven around to so many places in the city over the last couple of days.

After discovering the spray paint on his bedroom wall again, Corbray had searched his house, gun in hand. He made sure the house was empty, locked his doors, and immediately repainted the room once more. He only stopped between these activities to call his daughter and let her know he needed a place to stay for the night while his house was being fumigated.

He couldn't risk telling her the real reason he needed to vacate his house. Didn't want to let her know that he was scared of some crazy person out there who was stalking him. Didn't want to tell her that the previous night, upon discovery of the original spray paint, he had made an appointment to have a security system installed as soon as possible. The next morning, tomorrow, was the soonest appointment he could get.

When he had thought it was a practical joke, he hadn't minded waiting two nights in his house. But after having his property tread on, and, worse yet, having someone inside his house as he slept, he didn't want to risk reliving that experience again.

Telling his daughter the truth would lead to too many questions, none of which he could honestly answer. So, he simply told her that he had found a fly infestation upon coming home from his vacation and was getting the house taken care of right away. He said he thought it would give him the opportunity to catch up with his favourite daughter and grandson, a comment that made her laugh because they were his only daughter and grandson.

Morris and his ex-wife had had a child nearly a decade into their marriage. Sheila hadn't been planned for and was a shock to Mr. and Mrs. Corbray mainly because the couple had rarely had sex, which was the major reason their marriage had fallen apart. They had been okay friends for a married couple, but, at some point, his wife had decided that a mediocre cohabitation wasn't worth the constant feeling of rejection. An amicable marriage wasn't worth living with the dawning realization that the only way her husband was able to stay aroused by her was when he took her from behind with her face buried in a pillow.

Nearly fifteen years after parting ways the two were civil, though they only saw each other during the occasional holiday. More so since Riley, their grandson, had been born. Riley, who was currently watching television with his grandfather. Sitting on his lap.

Corbray looked around the living room of the small apartment, wondering when Sheila and her husband would advance in life. The place wasn't bad. It was quaint. It was cozy. Which meant it was cramped.

The Corruption of Philip Toles

Ideally, he would have called his contacts within The Fold and set himself up in a hotel, but he knew The Fold would ask him even more questions than Sheila if he had gone to them for assistance. And would have been insistent on truthful answers. He could have checked into a hotel himself, but they would have still been aware of it. And would have wondered why he hadn't taken advantage of what The Fold had to offer. Would have wondered why he was checking into a hotel so soon after coming back from New Eden.

As much as Corbray enjoyed being part of The Fold, especially after the vacation he'd just had, he understood that his life was no longer truly his. Had felt like someone had been following him since Kathleen had been shivved to death. Not every day, not always, but far too often for his liking. Headlights would trail behind him for far too long, for far too many lefts and rights to be a coincidence. He felt as though eyes would sometimes follow him when he was out in public. Whether it had been at work before he had retired, or at the mall, at the library, or visiting the grocers. Everywhere he went, he felt as though there was a possibility that he was being watched. He didn't dare ask Elareen about this. He understood she would respond with silence, and that would say it all.

Thankfully, he hadn't felt as though he'd been followed on his way to his daughter's house earlier on, and only hoped he wasn't bringing trouble to her and her little family.

Most of that family was here in their unit. He and Riley were watching TV while impatiently waiting for the boy's mother to announce that it was time for dinner. Spaghetti and meatballs. It was Corbray's favourite homecooked meal. He wasn't a difficult man to please when what he wanted was available. And he rarely left his daughter's house feeling less than satisfied.

Morris and his grandson watched Pat Sajak ask his contestants to spin the wheel and guess letters and enjoy their fifteen minutes of mostly local fame. A different sort of local fame than he had once been accustomed to. With the reminder of his own fifteen minutes having been plastered on his wall the day before, he could barely concentrate on what was happening in front of him. He kept wondering who it was that was targeting him. Potentially stalking him.

Disrupting his thoughts of the newspapers and his potential stalker was his daughter. He was thankful for that. While walking out from the kitchen carrying placemats and plates to their places on the modest dining room table, Sheila said,

"Andre just texted me back. He said he'll be staying at his parents' tonight. He has an early day tomorrow and it's less traffic to get to work from there."

She set down the placemats and plates, went back to the kitchen for cutlery. Corbray made noises from his closed mouth to acknowledge he had heard what his daughter had said. Heard it. Didn't believe it. Though he wasn't sure who was lying, his daughter or her husband.

He wasn't surprised, nor was he upset, that Andre, his son-in-law, suddenly had plans for this specific night. The young man seemed to always be conveniently elsewhere whenever Corbray came to visit.

The two men had never gotten along. If he were honest with himself, Corbray knew it was his fault. He'd been surprised when his daughter had introduced him to a black man. During Thanksgiving dinner, shortly after meeting Andre for the first time, Corbray had made a boorish comment he had meant to be a joke:

"Just make sure that if you two have kids you don't give them any of those ghetto names."

It had been understandably tense since then. Always awkward. Andre avoided his father-in-law whenever he could. This was something Corbray didn't mind at all. It only meant he got to spend more quality time with his grandson unimpeded. As he was now. Bouncing Riley on his lap.

"How are Andre's parents doing anyhow?" he decided to ask, though he couldn't have cared less.

"Oh, they're fine. His dad is going to be retiring in the next couple of years. Maybe you and him ought to sit down one of these days. You can tell him what to look forward to." She smiled at him as she re-entered the dining area, setting down the cutlery. He smiled back as he held little Riley close to him. The boy was rivetted by the spinning wheel on the television.

"That would be fun," he said, though there was nothing he would like to do less than see Andre's parents.

"Alright, boys! Dinner's ready!"

Riley gave a cry of excitement and slipped out of his grandfather's grasp, running the short distance through the living room to the dinner table.

"Give me a minute," Morris Corbray said, still on the couch, pretending to be going through his phone as he waited for his excitement at spending quality time with his grandson to become less obvious. Waited to settle down before he could risk standing up.

SEVEN o'clock was wake-up time at Sheila's house during weekdays. Her father, at this time, on this Tuesday morning, found himself roused from a very refreshing sleep by the alarm clock in his grandson's room.

He rolled over on the bed to check on the boy, but Riley must have gotten up before the alarm, which Corbray had been told was a failsafe in case 'mommy flubbed up and slept in,' as Sheila had put it the night before. Riley was always up before the device brayed, something that made his mother's life easier at times, but much less relaxing on mornings when he woke up too early, dragging her out of bed.

Corbray saw that today was one of those less relaxing mornings as he made his way to the kitchen after quickly dressing in the clothes he had worn the day before. Sheila was there, standing by the stove which had a frying pan on it. On the counter beside the stove was what looked to be the elements of what would make some sort of egg dish waiting to be put together in a specific way, heated and eaten. Riley was sitting at the dining table, his head halfway inside of a picture book about a family of falcons, patiently waiting for his breakfast.

"You guys are up and about early!" Morris said brightly. He stood at the entryway of the kitchen watching his little extended family, a warm smile on his face.

"Yeah, I couldn't sleep with all your snoring!" Riley said, before quickly turning his attention back to his book.

"And, of course, he had to wake me up to tell me *all* about it," Sheila chimed in, turning to make sure her father saw that she was rolling her eyes playfully at him.

"My apologies, my apologies. I'll be out of your hair right away."

"No rush, dad. I hope you're at least staying for breakfast. You can have Andre's share."

"You sure he won't be more annoyed with me than he already is?" he responded with a knowing chuckle.

"Dad!" Sheila said this in a whisper after turning and looking pointedly from her father to her son, indicating that this was not a conversation to be had in front of the young boy. "Andre's just not a very social creature. He needs his own space. That's all."

"Uh huh. Well, I can understand that. And I apologize. I know this has been an inconvenience for you all."

At that moment, Jar Jar waddled into the kitchen. He looked up and yipped at his owner, a clear indication that nature was calling him. The dog was a living point of emphasis on his statement of planning to head home immediately. Riley, upon seeing the terrier, nearly flung his book away in his haste to give Jar Jar a good morning hug.

"I'd like to stay but this guy has to go, if you know what I mean. Might as well hit the road if I'm going to be heading out there anyway."

"Is it safe at your house yet?"

"Pardon?" he said, startled by the question. Had he mentioned something to her about his recent troubles at the house? Did she suspect something?

"From the fumes. Is it safe to go back so soon?"

"Oh, yes," he said, almost forgetting the bogus reason he had given her for his visit. "I was assured it would be good to go as of this morning. It better be. I've got to get home and get focused and prepared. I have a big day ahead of me tomorrow. The start of a new chapter in my life."

"Oh, dad! I'm so sorry I forgot. You're starting with the youth group at your church! How are you feeling? Excited?" She was beaming at him. And he was glad at that. They may not have been as close as they once were, but she was still proud of him, and that meant the world to Morris.

"More excited than you know," he said honestly. "Nervous too. Being in the schools was fun, a real challenge at times, but I'm looking forward to a new challenge with a new group of students. Instead of trying to get kids to graduate to college, I'm trying to get them to graduate to Heaven. Slightly more pressure." They both laughed. When the laughter dissipated, Sheila looked at her father earnestly, lovingly. Said,

"You know what, dad? We really should do this more often. It doesn't have to be just in case of some bug-related emergency. Riley loves his grandpa, and Andre would warm up more to the idea of company as long as we don't spring it on him."

He smiled at his daughter, then looked at his grandson. Riley was on his knees on the kitchen floor playing with the dog.

"That sounds like a wonderful idea," Morris said, genuinely touched.

"And dad? You shouldn't be too stressed about the youth group. Everything's going to be great. You're going to be the best thing to happen to those kids!"

The Corruption of Philip Toles

****

Corbray felt good leaving his daughter's apartment. Refreshed. Almost optimistic. He said good morning to the people who rode down on the elevator with him. He didn't even have an issue with the old woman who went to rub Jar Jar's head. He was usually not the sort of person who liked strangers interacting with his dog, but this morning he didn't mind.

He felt grounded again. After spending quality time with his daughter and grandson, he felt able to think of the positives: his security system would be installed soon; he would officially be the new leader of a new group of kids within the next day; he was in good standing with Elareen and The Fold; if he remained in good standing with The Fold, then New Eden Isle and other wonders might be open to him on an annual basis.

So much to look forward to, he reminded himself as he and Jar Jar left the apartment building and walked out into the fresh morning air. It was cool, wet and windy, the weather report indicated it would be so for the next several days. But even the dour weather couldn't dampen his mood. He walked around the side of the building toward the visitor's parking lot, stopping by a row of leafless bushes to let Jar Jar do his business.

On Corbray's mind, at the moment, was the team of security installers set to arrive at his place during a three-hour window he hoped they would honour. On his mind was what he might have for lunch, not certain what he had in his fridge. On his mind were many mundane things he hoped would distract him from his issues.

Though, as he approached his car, he saw a distraction that wasn't very pleasant.

"Damn it all!" he said to himself softly but hotly, looking at his windshield from several feet away. "They can't ticket me for parking here. I'm allowed to be here until nine." He stomped over to his car, all his other issues suddenly forgotten. He hadn't yet realized it because of his anger at the notion of being ticketed, but something like this had the potential to be the perfect distraction. Exactly what he needed.

Until it wasn't.

After letting Jar Jar into the vehicle, Corbray grabbed the white piece of paper pinned to the windshield beneath his wiper. He turned it to see what was written on the other side, and nearly let it drop and blow away in the wind when what was on it became apparent. Because what he saw on the paper shook him greatly. Shook him to his core. And from there all the way to his now trembling fingers.

It wasn't a ticket. It was a leaflet.

On it, in bold black letters, the words:

STOP THE EXPLOITATION OF CHILDREN!

Corbray whirled around, wondering if someone was watching him even now. Wondering if, somehow, someone had been watching him last night.

No chance, he thought. *A coincidence,* he said to himself.

He examined the other vehicles in the visitor's parking lot. Not a single one had a white flyer on its windshield.

His eyes went back to the leaflet, looking at it more closely this time. The photo on it, beneath the bold black words, was one he remembered.

He was looking at a picture of Rosenthal P. Straily Public School.

The Corruption of Philip Toles

Recognizing that photo caused him to recognize the leaflet entirely. It was a bit of literature that had been distributed around town not long after Philip had been found dead. One of many flyers that had spoken out against the school and the school board, blaming the faculty for not taking a firm enough stance against Kathleen Jeffreys. Criticizing the staff for choosing initially to suspend rather than fire her. And for not vocally chastising her in the media, presenting instead carefully crafted statements that had used many words to say nothing.

Morris Corbray remembered it well.

He only wished he knew why this piece of paper from the past was here now. Why any of this was happening after all these years.

He quickly folded the flyer and shoved it in his pocket. Then, after diligently checking his car, looking in the backseat, even popping the trunk and very hesitantly peering inside, he got behind the wheel. Corbray sat there until his nerves were steady enough to allow his hands to steer the vehicle. Before he drove off, he looked around the area outside of his car again to see if anyone suspicious was in sight. Feeling exceptionally paranoid, he checked his backseat a second time. It was empty except for Jar Jar, who looked at his master curiously.

He kept thinking of all the horror movies he had seen. The ones where the ghoul sprang out from behind the unsuspecting driver. He thought of the Mafia movies he had watched with the gangster hiding in the backseat, garrote in hand, bad intentions in heart.

He was thinking of unfinished business. Of retribution. And wondering, as he slowly drove home, just who might be hoping to attain a measure of vengeance on him.

****

Later that day, back at his house, Corbray contemplated the last week of his life as he sat in his study going over what he would say during the following evening's youth group meeting. His vacation had legitimately been the best time of his life. What had followed immediately after felt like the worst. Now, with a new security system installed and the positive boost he had received from visiting his daughter and grandchild, he was doing his best to put all the negative that had happened over the last couple of days out of his mind.

He burned the flyer he had found on his car shortly after the alarm installers had left. Torched it in his kitchen sink. He'd taken a small measure of pleasure from the task. As he had watched it turn to ash, he was comforted by the fact that it wouldn't simply up and vanish later on like the newspapers had.

As he had watched it burn, he'd hoped the gesture of torching something from his past was more than just symbolic. Had hoped the smoldering piece of literature would be the end of this ordeal. Had reminded himself that he was home. He was safe. And now, due to his new system, he was as secure as he had ever been.

He repeated those reminders to himself now as he focused on his daughter's words from earlier that day. Told himself that everything was going to be great. That this would be the start of a fantastic new chapter.

He thought of the youth group, thought of the church. Thought of how wonderful this latest phase of his life might be. Morris Corbray sipped his wine and allowed himself to relax in his home for the first time since leaving that magical island.

EIGHT p.m. approached very slowly for Morris Corbray. He sat nervously, every so often looking at the clock on the wall of the room he was in. In that room with him were twelve others. Seven boys and four girls between the ages of twelve and seventeen. Youths. Another adult was present with them in this room in the basement of the Courtville community church. A church called New Beginnings. A name Corbray had found perfectly apt when he had decided to make this place a part of his future.

He was currently a spectator along with the youths as the second adult there, Deacon James, spoke to the room. Answering questions they had about life, about changes and inevitable ends. Rapid-fire citing quotes from the Bible that helped the deacon add heavenly support to the responses he provided them. Corbray knew he had his work cut out for him when it came to replacing the deacon. He wasn't particularly religious. His priest had done things to him when he was a child that had pushed the God out of him.

Corbray had been confused for some time during his days as a youth, had hated his priest for a while. Now he wished he could ask his old priest for advice. On scripture. On many things.

He was feeling increasingly intimidated by Deacon James's performance with each passing moment. He tried to remind himself that he didn't have to memorize the Bible to be effective at this task. His skill was being able to identify a child's issues, to know what was wrong even when the child didn't. To provide guidance. He could memorize a quote or two of scripture for effect along the way.

They sat in chairs in a room that reminded him of one of the old, outdated classrooms from his days at Rosenthal P. Straily. Deacon James stood in front of a chalkboard delivering what would be his final lesson as the leader of the youth group. Preparing to pass the baton to Corbray, who would run with it from this day forward.

The two men had spoken of this meeting, which currently seemed to be evoking much emotion from the youth around them, since it had been announced during Sunday service months ago that Deacon James would be moving on. And that one of the newest, most involved and most giving members of the church would be taking over the youth group. There had been both sadness and delight from the congregation. No one liked the idea of Deacon James slowing down and getting too old for the duties he adored, but everyone was happy to see the well-liked Morris Corbray take a more active role with the children of the church.

And now, they were finally here. The meeting was approaching its halfway point, nearing eight o'clock. The plan was for Deacon James to introduce Corbray at the top of the hour and allow him to take a more active role alongside the deacon for the second half of the meeting. Deacon James was set to be at the next meeting as well, though he would take a more passive role as Corbray ran the class from start to finish. Then, Corbray would be in charge of things all on his own thereafter. It was sure to be a smooth transition.

He took a deep breath, feeling more nervous than he expected himself to be. He reminded himself again of what his daughter had told him.

Things are going to go great, he repeated internally.

"And now," Deacon James said from the front of the class. The portly, baldheaded man in glasses was all smiles. "Your wonderful new counsellor, friend and leader of this program, Youth Minister Morris Corbray will say some words and lead us in prayer."

"Thank you, Deacon James," the newly minted Youth Minister Corbray said, walking to the front of the room. After shaking hands with his predecessor, he turned to the small group of students. There were only eleven of them now because it was a school night, but there would be a greater turnout in two nights, on Friday, when there was no impending day of school the next morning. He looked at each of them, evaluating, checking for signs of brokenness that he might be able to help in his own special way. Help by directing them into the hands of The Fold. Into The Lifestyle.

He couldn't wait to see the rest of them. Couldn't wait to get to know them all.

"It will be hard to follow such a great man as Deacon James," Minister Corbray stated to the youth, still scanning their faces, the room. "But I will do my best to fill you with the spirit of G... Guh... God... Ohmygod..."

The statement dissolved into uncertainty, the end of it barely a whisper as Minister Corbray's eyes landed upon the door. The closed door with the glass window set in it.

Beyond that window, looking in, was a face. Another youthful face.

If not for the red hat above that face, Mr. Corbray might have allowed himself to believe it was just some young boy too embarrassed to enter the room after being extremely late. Might have only given him a glance before returning his attention to the rest of the class. If not for the fact that he had seen this same red hat only a matter of days ago, in all of those newspapers, he might have ignored the boy.

But he *had* seen those newspapers, and he did recognize the old red special edition Blue Jays hat which had been photographed during a fishing trip nearly fifteen years ago. The baseball cap the boy wore nearly every day at school. The hat that had been found beneath his feet on the gymnasium floor on the day he had been discovered hanging. Found dead.

It was impossible. Illogical.

But there it was. The same baseball cap, and, impossibly, illogically, it seemed to be the same boy beneath it.

Looking in at the church youth group, grim faced, unmoving, unblinking, not seeming to breathe, staring at no one and nothing but Youth Minister Morris Corbray, was Philip Toles.

"God... God help me..."

Minister Corbray continued to whisper to a God whose institution he had exploited for his own selfish desires while believing that the Devil himself had come to claim him here and now.

NINE o'clock took a year to arrive that evening.

Or so it felt to Youth Minister Corbray. That final hour of the youth meeting was testimony to the theory of time being a relative thing. A fickle creature. Something that stretched slowly and strolled sloth-like when it was needed to speed along.

After the boy at the door – *not Philip, it couldn't really have been Philip* – had walked away, and Minister Corbray had apologized, blaming his nerves for the interruption, he had shakily recited the prayer he had intended to begin his tenure as minister with. Afterward, the youths had asked him questions about what they should expect from him. About what from the Bible he valued most. Questions that he had prepared to answer for months but was inadequately prepared to answer on this night because seeing the boy in the red hat – whoever he was – had thrown him off so badly.

Now, twenty minutes after leaving the church, he was standing on his porch in front of his front door.

He had raced out of the youth meeting nearly immediately after it ended, foregoing the usual small talk and chit chat with the stragglers and brown-nosers by telling them he wasn't feeling well. No one had reason to doubt this after seeing how out of it he had been since standing up to read the prayer.

He had nearly run to his car, but he managed to force himself to walk toward it slowly and cautiously, examining the area around him and his vehicle as it came into his sight.

After checking to make sure the car was empty, and not occupied by some (impossible and illogical) child wearing a red hat, he had driven off, raced home, every so often checking his rear-view mirror to make sure he hadn't missed a vengeful spirit in his backseat that might aim to claim him as he drove.

After all of that leaving immediately and speeding to get home, he simply stood at his door, terrified to open it. Not knowing what would be in store for him next. He had been standing there for several minutes, not sure what to do. He was briefly grateful that he didn't have any neighbours in close proximity. Someone looking at a man standing there staring absently at the front door might have taken him for a reluctant robber, an unwanted person in their midst. Though following that thought was one which detailed how nice it might be to have neighbours once in a while. In case he had to cry out for help. To run from danger.

"You're being silly, Corbray," he said to himself. "It was a kid who was too embarrassed to walk into class. That's why he walked away when you made eye contact. He didn't know what to do. Lots of kids wear shitty red hats. Your mind just made him out to look like Philip on account of what the prankster and their newspapers have been putting you through."

He had been saying or thinking this, or portions of this, or variations of this, since getting into his car and trying to process what had just happened. What had been happening. What could still be happening.

He took several deep breaths, none of which did anything to calm his racing heart.

There was a slight shock, enough to make him jump, when he opened the door and heard it. His newly installed security alarm informing him in a robotic voice that this house was armed. As though the entire structure might rise up and shoot a potential intruder.

He still wasn't accustomed to it. If not for the fact that he was a man of many secrets, he likely wouldn't have locked his door at all, let alone gotten a security system. Many of the people who lived in this area didn't bother with their locks. He had pondered it, but hadn't seriously considered getting a security system until the ugly joke someone had played on him. Now, on a night when his nerves were wrought, he was more certain than ever it had been the correct move.

Still, as he walked into the house he felt unsettled, like something was off. Some energy in the air out of alignment. Momentarily disrupting his dour thoughts was the sound of little rapidly moving feet approaching him in the dark as he was reaching for the light switch. He was glad to hear them.

"Hey Jar Jar!" he said to the dog once the light was on, kneeling down to pet his pet, thankful the dog was okay and unbothered.

Of course he's okay. It was a prank. And now you have an alarm system and no one can get in. It's over, he said to himself. To the dog, he said,

"And *you're* the best alarm system anyone could have, aren't you boy? If you'd been here instead of at the kennel, that asshole wouldn't have gotten in here with all those nasty newspapers, would he? No, he wouldn't've. Oh no he wouldn't..." He baby talked to the dog, lying to Jar Jar about his security prowess for no real reason other than to say something comforting. Ignoring the fact that Jar Jar had been in the house the second time the intruder had painted the walls. He rubbed his best friend's head, kissing the creature and letting the dog lick his lips as Jar Jar's tail wagged rapidly in obvious agreement with everything his master was saying.

****

As midnight approached, Youth Minister Corbray found himself in his study listening to music, though at a much lower volume than usual. He was accompanied by a bottle of rye and a tumbler he was refilling too frequently. In addition to these items, on his desk, was his laptop, which was what had occupied his evening.

He had been searching. For answers. For Philip.

He wasn't certain why, but he had sat down, Googled the boy's name and then begun reading. And drinking. And searching. And reading and drinking as the night was lost inside the glow created by his fifteen-inch screen.

Perhaps he had wanted to see if there was some new break in the case, some uproar around Philip Toles that might send trouble his way. He kept thinking back to the television shows and news stories he had seen of cold case files getting hot beneath unsuspecting culprits. He couldn't help but wonder if that might be his fate. But all seemed quiet. If the police had anything new, he reasoned to himself, he was certain Elareen would have told him. Or perhaps he would be dead already. No, the more he searched the web the more confident he was that the newspapers, the leaflet, all of it had been a sick joke.

His search eventually devolved from one of attaining new information to one of reviewing information he had already known, information that had recently been in his house in the form of a plethora of newspapers containing the names and faces in print that he was looking at online now. He allowed himself the trip down memory lane. It was jarring to see all of these details again, to be reminded specifically of how long ago it all was.

He read about the discovery of Philip's body, the media frenzy that followed, he scrolled and scanned through his own statements and interviews, and he went over what seemed to be the final chapter of Philip's story in the detailing of the murder of his teacher and rapist in a prison yard.

There had been general satisfaction felt by the citizens of Saturn City when the news of Kathleen's murder had been made public way back then. For some people it had been cause for outright celebration, her death bringing about a feeling of finality. Of justice. The person responsible for her murder had been hailed a hero.

The whole situation with Philip had been nasty, ugly, and had turned an entire community upside down. Corbray understood his role in it, but, even now, felt as though it had been necessary. Not only necessary, but beneficial.

He thought of New Eden, of the beaches. Of the boys.

He took a drink and toasted Philip, the child who had changed his life. Noticing the date on his computer, he toasted the very thing he had been taunted by while tearing and bunching and disposing of those now vanished newspapers: Philip's birthday.

The anniversary of the day his body had been found, October sixteenth, was this Friday.

Only two days away.

Knowing the anniversary was coming up only helped to strengthen Corbray's conviction that what had happened since returning from his vacation was someone's idea of a gag. There had been anger at the entire school staff for allowing a boy to be involved with and to impregnate a teacher. And then to subsequently die because of that involvement.

Many of the teachers had been slandered, barraged with hate from the community. One of those community members, some loon, must have realized that it had been thirteen years since Philip's thirteenth birthday. A birthday the boy never got to experience. That crazy person likely wanted members of the staff to remember what he or she deemed them responsible for. That was all, that was it, Corbray convinced himself. It wasn't the first time a stranger had sought him out over their interest in Philip and his story.

He recalled reporters reaching out to see if he wanted to speak about Philip or Kathleen when the anniversary of either of their deaths was coming up. This was during those early years after all that had transpired. Around that same time, he had been asked by a television network to be interviewed for an expose related to sex crimes, he being perceived as an expert after working so closely to a monster like Kathleen Jeffreys.

There might have been a time when he would have said yes to any or all the invitations to stretch his fifteen minutes of fame into more, but he had declined all offers to speak on any topics linked to Philip after Kathleen had been killed. Not only would it have been unwise, but Elareen had forbade it.

It was possible that after all these years, people were still as interested as they had once been in Philip's story. Maybe one of those people was still upset. The mean jokes Corbray had been experiencing over the last few days might just be their way of expressing that upset. Corbray was satisfied with this line of reasoning. He only hoped the crazy person responsible for the pranks had gotten their kicks out of his brief misery. Hoped that they could all move on.

He looked at the pictures online again, pausing on the one with Philip in the baseball cap several times.

It was different, he told himself. *Different hat, different kid. You're letting that crazy person get to you.*

He continued to drink and scroll until he got his fill of looking into the past. Silently, he toasted Philip again, then logged onto a different website. One which required a person to confirm that they were above eighteen years of age though may not necessarily have asked the same of those whose images and videos were all over the site.

Minutes later, content and with Jar Jar by his side, Corbray shut down his computer, turned off his light and went to go to his bedroom after briefly stopping in the bathroom to wash his hands.

He paused outside his bedroom door. Hesitated to enter the room. It was at this point he remembered the black paint that had been on his walls. Ugly black words he had painted over twice. What if they were back again?

You have a security system now, he reminded himself. Then came a smaller, drunken, absurd thought. One which sparked a fear in him that chilled:

Security systems don't work on ghosts.

He dismissed the thought outright, then opened the door, his need for rationality overcoming his fear. Feigning confidence in hopes that he would feel it, he walked in boldly. Turned on the lights. Looked at the wall.

No words. Just a fresh, slightly pungent smelling coat of beige paint.

His relief caused him to smile as Youth Minister Corbray fell into bed without bothering to change out of his clothes, hoping that the madness was behind him. Optimistic that this would be one of many peaceful nights to come.

Ten minutes later, he was asleep.

TEN minutes later, he was awake. Awoken.

It was the sound of a bang that had brought Corbray slightly out of sleep not long after he had drifted off on his bed, still in his clothes from the youth group meeting. It was a one-off sound, he thought to himself sleepily. Maybe something falling, perhaps a branch against the front of the house. He began to drift back to sleep when that sound was followed by another:

"This house is armed!" his system said sternly in stereo sound.

Then another bang.

This was followed by the system counting down. The system counting with more urgency.

Another bang.

Then the countdown was over. The security alarm screamed into the night.

The sound of the alarm woke him fully, the feeling of alarm made him leap straight out of bed. His gun found its way into his hand before he even realized he had reached for the drawer of the nightstand he'd placed it in earlier. He was operating on automatic, driven by panic and the hope that this wasn't his crazy tormentor come back to redo the walls once again, only this time with his blood.

"Who's there?" he said, despite knowing that calling out was pointless with the sound of the alarm braying. He considered staying upstairs. In less than a minute the voice of a live agent would ring out through the speakers, letting whoever might have been there know the police were on their way.

That would be the safer option. That would be the option someone could take if they didn't have the past he had. The connections. The stash of child pornography hidden in his shed and on his laptop. He didn't want the police here. The alarm was to make him aware of intruders, and it was doing that job now. If he could handle the situation on his own without the authorities present, that would be best.

Steeling himself, pointing the gun in front of him like he had seen in so many Hollywood cop movies, never feeling more like a feeble retiree in his life, Corbray hurried out of the room.

He always kept the hallway light on, and this time was thankful for it. Because he could see that there was no one there. As he looked down the stretch of hall, he regretted for the first time having such an unnecessarily large house. Why did he need two floors? Why did he need so many rooms on this floor alone? The doors to those rooms stood open, dark and hollow like the mouths of giant beasts waiting to consume him.

He forced himself to move forward quickly, the alarm still sounding. Corbray was determined to get to the door and turn it off as fast as he could. Then deal with whoever might be here by himself.

He made his way down the stairs rapidly but cautiously, his left hand reaching across his body to slide along the railing, giving his shaky legs support while his right hand - also shaky – aimed his gun toward the door.

If someone was inside, that person had politely closed the door behind them, though he could see they hadn't locked it. He raced to the front door, locked it and turned off the alarm in time to prevent the authorities from being dispatched. Reactivated the system. If the intruder was outside, they were hopefully fleeing, scared off by the alarm. If they were inside, well, Corbray wouldn't mind introducing this new nuisance to his pistol. Teach them a lesson about boundaries.

"Jar Jar?" he called to his dog. When there was no immediate response, he found a new fear. One that was quickly assuaged when little feet came padding and scratching along the floor, coming to the foyer from the living room by way of the kitchen. The single seater in the living room was another of Jar Jar's sleeping spots. He had likely been terrified by all the commotion.

The dog meekly took up a place beside his owner, walking alongside Corbray as he first checked the kitchen, then the living room. Backtracked, checked his entire house. Then repeated the process, opening each room and searching every cranny and closet, each turn of a corner making him feel as though a heart attack was inevitable this night. But, after some time, his heart stopped beating with such force and speed. The adrenaline wore off. He felt his muscles – particularly those in his arms, which had been raising his gun for several uninterrupted minutes – starting to become heavier. It was the effect of him calming down, of the awareness that there was no intruder inside of the house.

When his heartrate felt like it was close to normal, he went back to the front door, going to doublecheck that the alarm was on, that the door was locked.

He had a feeling then. An inkling. Some interior urge telling him to open the door. To look out.

Which was what he did.

The first thing he noticed was the wind. It was forceful, nearly blowing his door into him the moment he opened it.

Could it have been the wind? he wondered. *Maybe I didn't shut the door when I got in, and that's what was making all that banging.* He wanted to believe it, but two things were causing him not to.

The first was that, in his hyper paranoid state, he would not have left the door unlocked, let alone not properly shut.

The second and most important thing causing his disbelief was that, after walking into the windy night, standing on his porch and looking down the road, Corbray was almost certain, as he squinted into the dark, that he was looking at a figure standing there. Someone motionless in the middle the road. A silhouette in the moonlight.

If someone was there, they were standing perfectly still. *If* someone was there, Corbray couldn't tell which direction that someone might have been looking, but knew, was sure, that *if* someone was there, they were looking straight at him. Observing. Asking him to continue to play this game.

Corbray pointed his pistol at the maybe someone-maybe shadow. Contemplated shooting. Thought better of it.

Instead, he went inside, locked the door, and activated his alarm again. Then checked once more to make sure that every other door and window was locked before heading upstairs to his bedroom where he would try, but likely fail, to sleep.

ELEVEN days had gone by since Morris Corbray had thought his future was a bright and sunny place. Eleven days ago, he had taken off to New Eden Isle at the expense of The Fold. A present. A promotion. A new level of life that men of his previous profession usually never ascended to. All because he had somehow stumbled into being valuable. And had remained so for over a decade.

Now, standing by his front door the morning after pointing his pistol at a phantom in the dark, he understood that his future might be a dismal destination. It was the first time he had experienced anything close to despair or hopelessness since feeling Elareen's scarf (which he had since learned was essentially a cloth covered bullwhip) around his wrist all those years prior. Despite his life belonging to The Fold since then, this was the first time he felt as though it was completely out of his control. Because this was the only time since meeting Elareen that he was reminded there might be real and immediate consequences to his actions.

The first of those consequences being the terrible thing he had woken up to that morning, eleven minutes before now.

Currently, after scrambling for that eleven minutes, after being beside himself, and while still being despondent, his cell phone began to ring. He looked at it.

It was his daughter, or so the caller ID display stated. He considered ignoring it. Corbray was still distraught over what he had discovered eleven minutes ago. He wasn't sure he would be able to keep the emotion out of his voice. And it wasn't as though he could share his worries with his daughter. He knew it was unwise to answer in the state he was in, but he suddenly very much needed to hear a loving voice. He cleared his throat, settled his emotions, answered the call.

"Hey, honey. Didn't expect to hear from you so soon. Those pesky flies have all been taken ca—"

"Mr. Corbray? It's Andre, not Sheila." It was an accented voice. One that sounded, to Mr. Corbray, like a confusing mixture of some place in Africa and another in Britain. It was not the voice he was expecting to hear. It was the voice of his son-in-law.

Suddenly he felt like his decision to answer the call was about to make an already bad morning even worse.

"Oh..." he said, genuinely dumbfounded. He couldn't remember a single time he had been called directly by the young man. At least not in the last few years. If they ever spoke, it was usually after Sheila called and briefly put the phone on speaker if her husband was present. A quick 'Hello', 'How are you?'. Platitudes. Never a call practically first thing in the morning.

"Are Sheila and Riley okay?" Mr. Corbray asked, unable to think of any other possible reason Andre could be calling him.

"Yes, they're fine... It's just that..." Mr. Corbray could hear Andre struggling to sort out what he wanted to say. He could also hear his daughter in the background saying something that sounded like, "Honestly, Andre, it's not a big deal." He heard Andre take a deep breath, exhale shaky words.

"I'm going to be as straight forward as I can, sir. My son said you slept in his bed the other night when you were here. *In* his bed. *With* him. Is that right?"

"Oh..." Mr. Corbray said again. Then thought, *Fuck*, before quickly saying, "Honestly, I didn't think anything of it. The boy has a large bed and the floor was hurting my back."

"We have a pull-out couch, sir."

"No offense, Andre, but the mattresses on those things are never comfortable. That would have been even worse than the floor."

"You know, there are plenty of hotels all over the city that have really nice beds that would have been plenty good for your back," Andre retorted quickly. It sounded like the reminder of hotels was something he might have already brought up to Sheila several times before making this call.

There was what would have been a silent pause, if not for Sheila in the background admonishing her husband. Telling him to be more polite to her father. Telling him, again, and this time Mr. Corbray heard it clearly, that it wasn't a big deal.

"Are you stating that I'm not welcome in my daughter's home, Andre?" He was trying to sound firm, authoritative, undaunted, but he was terrified. Not only because of this phone call but because of what he had woken up to several minutes ago. His voice quivered ever so slightly, betraying the façade he was trying to create.

"No, sir. What I'm saying is that you're not welcome in my son's bed." Andre sighed. It was the sound of rage slowly seeping from his system. Mr. Corbray could tell the young man was struggling to calm himself as he continued on.

"I never thought I would have to say that, and I never want to have to say it again. Are we clear?"

"Of course! But Andre, I just want you to know that I would never, *ever* do anything that would make Riley feel uncomfortable." He finished this statement even though halfway through it he had gotten a sense that there would be no reply.

Andre, his son-in-law, had hung up the phone on him.

He thought about calling back but thought better of it. Understood that, if that phone call, that bit of a tongue lashing, was the worst consequence to come out of the little sleepover he'd had with his grandson, then he could consider himself lucky. He quickly pushed thoughts of his daughter and her family out of his mind.

At that moment, he had more pressing matters to be concerned with.

"Jar Jar!" he called out again into the empty house from his foyer. And once again there was no yipping response, no skittering of feet on the floor from elsewhere in the house.

Before receiving the call from Andre, Corbray had come in from outside where he had been calling out for his dog while briefly jogging back and forth along the stretch of road leading to his property. The same stretch of road that someone might have been standing on while watching him the night before. Now he worried as he wondered if that shadowy someone might have broken into his house somehow – somehow without tripping the alarm – and abducted his dog. His best friend.

"Jar Jar!" he cried despairingly into the hollow house. It must have been the thousandth time he'd said the dog's name since realizing he was gone.

He distinctly remembered seeing Jar Jar, and having the dog trot beside him the night before. Jar Jar had been scared after the alarm had gone off. Then Corbray had gone to confront a shadow and... he couldn't remember if he had seen Jar Jar after that.

Had the shadow snuck into his house somehow without tripping the alarm? It was unlikely. It was more likely that the dog had followed him outside the night before and Mr. Corbray, in his idiotic, fearful frame of mind, had locked his poor pet outside.

Since discovering Jar Jar gone, he'd quickly searched his house, scanned the area in front of it and down the road. Had come back inside only to grab his car keys in order to search the entirety of his neighbourhood. He was about to do just that, until he remembered he hadn't checked the backyard.

The back door had remained locked all night, but the dog could have gone around the house into the backyard after finding himself locked out the night before. If that is what had happened to him.

In his fervent desperation, Corbray ran out to his backyard, nearly crashing through the glass doors leading there from his kitchen. Once outside, he saw something he did not want to see.

"Noooo!" was the first word from him when his eyes registered what was in front of him. What he was seeing hanging from one of the apple trees in his yard.

He ran to the tree. Raced to the leash that was dangling from it, blowing in the yet-to-settle winds. By the time he reached it he was in tears at what had been left there for him to find. To make sense of.

A nail to the heart. That was what he was seeing, and that was how this felt.

The dog's heart-shaped identification tag was fixed to the tree, nailed to it. The dog's leash was attached to the ID tag, hanging from it. Beneath the leash and atop the fallen leaves on the ground was the dog's collar. Usually black, there was a dried reddish-brown substance smeared on part of it.

He looked at the leash as it twisted and danced in the ominous breeze. There was no dog attached to it.

Jar Jar had been stolen, taken. Vanished.

"Jar Jar, no!" Mr. Corbray cried out, then sank to his knees before the tree, crying, bemoaning his dog's disappearance. Lamenting that somehow this tormentor had entered his life.

And, even as he imagined what merciless things that monster might be doing to his dog, he couldn't help but wonder what cruelties they might have in store for him next.

TWELVE drinks after he had discovered the dogless dog leash dangling from his tree – three hours in real time – Morris Corbray was still trying to come to terms with his life and what all of this would mean for him. He was no longer drinking but guzzling, foregoing his wine, his tumbler; pulling out a previously rarely used shot glass and filling it with rye.

Emptying it, then filling it again. Then again.

Shots, shots, shots.

He was building up the courage to do something he never believed he would ever do.

Someone had taken his dog. This was undoubtable. It wasn't the wind or a shadow. It wasn't his imagination. Someone, or some entity, had been in his house after he had searched it, locked his door, and turned on the alarm. Someone had entered noiselessly, not only taking the dog, but also taking Jar Jar's collar and leash which were kept on the rustic console table in the hallway near the front door.

Someone had been in and out of his house, had made a crude display on his tree as though they were marking it. Some beast had come to claim what was Morris Corbray's. Starting with his dog. And ending... where?

His freedom? His life?

He contemplated many things – his dog, his future, his current situation – as he sat in his study after finishing drink twelve.

His gun was in front of him. On the desk.

Once again, he had a decision to make.

As difficult as it would be, he understood that he had reached a new low. He had considered many options, but knew there was no other way out.

He reached down to his desk.

Picked up the phone beside the pistol.

Searched through his contacts until he found 'E16'.

And, on this ruinous morning, Morris Corbray placed a call to Elareen, The Beast in the Night.

She answered the phone after barely a ring.

"Corbray," she said. "What can I do for you?"

This was how she always addressed him whenever they interacted. Never a hello. After all these years, she had yet to use his first name. There was never any emotion in her voice when he heard it, no concern whenever she answered one of the few calls he had made to her. She simply stated his last name and asked him what he wanted. It always felt as if the saying of his name, the way it was said, was like her turning on a very brief timer and expecting him to be done saying what he had to say before it ran down.

He cut to it.

"I think... I think I'm in some trouble. Someone might know."

"Might know what?"

"You know. *Might*... Might *know*..."

There was a stretch of silence. This was always the case during conversations with Elareen. He understood by now without a doubt that these were not contemplative silences.

He believed them to be purposefully painful. A tiny taste of torture.

He wanted to press her for words but knew that would be a mistake. Instead, he waited as she wanted him to, reminding him without a sound that, even in his panic, this was her time. Time itself, his life, the potential relief to this panic he was in. It was all hers.

"Do you recall the first gift I gave you, Mr. Corbray? Other than the opportunity to improve your life and standing?"

He looked down at the pistol in front of him. Confirmed to her that he remembered.

"Clean it, oil it, make sure that it is still functional..."

"Yes? Then?" he asked, this time hoping to curtail the coming silence with an immediate question, though he knew she wasn't fond of those. But his strategy seemed to work on this occasion because she responded right away.

"...Then perhaps you should use it," Elareen said.

Then she said nothing. Then he heard nothing.

A different sort of silence.

He stayed there with the phone to his ear even though he knew no one was on the other end.

He tried to call her back but there was no answer.

He tried again several more times consecutively.

No ring tone. No voicemail.

He called Elareen once more after waiting an eternal ten minutes.

This time there was an answer.

A mechanical voice. A recording:

"The phone number you are trying to reach is no longer in service..."

Morris Corbray put the phone down. Picked the bottle up. Poured and swallowed drink thirteen.

THIRTEEN years old. That was the age Philip Toles would have turned on the day they found his body. On this day. This day, thirteen years ago.

Today was Philip's birthday. The anniversary of the day he had been found hanging. Hanged.

Morris Corbray, upon waking up at his desk, may have remembered this significant date on his own, but he wasn't allowed to. Because he was woken up to, and by, a very stark reminder of it.

He had been woken by the sound of noise. People's voices. Singing.

"Happy birthday to you..."

The sound drifted up the stairs, easily sliding into his study and past the door he had both closed and locked before passing out. The door that was now wide open.

"Happy birthday to you..."

He wanted to ignore it, to go back to sleep. He was incredibly tired. Part of the reason for his exhaustion was because his dreams had been ill. In his nightmares, he had been at Foster's Family Restaurant.

He had been at his usual booth looking at an unusual waitress. Unusual to him, unusual in general.

She was beautiful by any measure, attractive even to someone who wasn't attracted to her sort. She was young, somewhere between a teenager and a young adult. She had braces, and eyes so blue they looked neon in the dim restaurant lighting. In her raven-black hair danced a small black bird.

The waitress was naked except for the words written all over her body. Black ink all over her bloodred skin.

He recognized those words. They were items from the menu. Most of the items that he knew were never actually served in the restaurant.

"Welcome to Foster's. May I take your order, sir?" the young Red Lady asked. He remembered, in this nightmare, wanting to say no. Instead, his mouth moved, and he said,

"Pickled beef heart."

She had said, "Yes sir." And in her hand, where there wasn't one before, appeared a carving knife. She turned the knife to the area between her breasts, where the menu item was written. As he watched, unable to move or speak, the girl had begun to carve. To excavate.

In his dream he had winced, expecting blood. Instead, what came out of the girl as she separated skin and tissue, cut through breastbone, was bright Blue Fog the same colour as her eyes, billowing like smoke from a chimney.

"May I take your order, sir?" She said again after placing Her bloodless black heart on the table. He had wanted to say, 'No thank you, the heart is plenty enough.' Instead, he said,

"Steak tartare." And Her knife had gone to Her stomach.

He had ordered several items, each of which had been placed upon his table. He'd been horrified by these. Organs. Offal. Until he realized that this was not the true horror.

What terrified him most was not what She had lost of Herself, what he had forced Her to remove, to lose. What terrified him most was what had become of The Red Lady's torso.

He saw wide wounds, gaping holes, exposed cavities.

From those openings shone a crimson light that seemed to chase away the Blue Fog. A light that looked, to Corbray, like Bright Red Madness.

Inside that light, inside the wounds, with the organs cleared away, Corbray could see hands with fingers like worms. An unreasonable amount of them. Wringing and wrapping around each other, creeping over one another, crawling to the edges of her wounds, poking out of them as though these fingers were peeking. Searching. Eager for release. Eager to touch.

Reaching for him. Reaching...

Then the singing had woken him up.

"Happy birthday, dear Philip... Happy birthday to you!"

There was applause after the birthday song was sung. This was followed by indistinguishable words before the singing started again.

He was now wide awake. How could he not be? If his ears were to be believed, there was a birthday party going on in his household at – he looked over at the clock on the wall – 4:04 a.m. But he wasn't sure if he could believe his ears, his eyes, or any of his senses based on all that had happened since he had returned home from his trip. A trip that had been a visit to Heaven on Earth before he had been deposited in this Hell. And here was a fresh level for him to descend to.

"Happy birthday to you..."

He reached into the drawer of his desk in search of his pistol after realizing it wasn't resting in front of him on the desk's surface. If he hadn't been fully awake a moment before doing this, he became wide awake when his hand dipped into the drawer and felt only papers, paper clips. Nothing to kill with.

Not quite trusting his hand, he looked into the drawer.

Opened the one below, touched and looked. Then the third drawer, same process once more. And once more, the same result: no pistol.

The people downstairs continued to sing.

He checked the top of his desk in case he had somehow missed seeing a firearm sitting there. He hadn't. It was still missing. Someone had taken it. Someone had stood there in front of him with his gun in their hand as he slept.

He felt a chill run through him.

Maybe you left the room and put it somewhere while you were drunk, he tried to convince himself. But he didn't believe the thought. He had spent the previous day drinking while pacing his house. Worried about his dog, daughter, and life. He only experienced relief from one of those concerns when Sheila had called to apologize for her husband's behaviour. Corbray had quickly accepted the apology before returning to drinking. And pacing and worrying until he eventually passed out in his office. The entire time, he had kept his pistol on him. It was the only thing he felt would keep him safe in this situation.

Calling the police was no longer an option. Not when Elareen had excommunicated him. The moment he called the cops, it would be certain suicide. Violently assisted. He would wind up like Mrs. Jeffreys, punctured and drained until dead. Left somewhere to rot like so much rubbish. Like he himself had left the body of a young boy named Philip. A young boy who was being sung to right now, in Corbray's house. A young boy whose memory he couldn't escape or elude.

"Happy birthday to you..."

Even if he wanted to call the police, he realized he literally could not. Both his cell phone and the cordless landline he kept in his office were nowhere to be found. They were gone along with his gun.

"Happy birthday, dear Philip..."

Corbray grabbed a letter opener from the 'World's Greatest Grandpa' mug on his desk, in which he kept his pens and pencils and things that might be used to stab someone with under desperate circumstances. The mug had been a gift from his daughter when she had announced that she was having Riley. He wondered, if all of his sins came to light, what she would think about the grandfather of her child then.

Feeling like someone else was in control of his legs – legs which suddenly weighed, each of them, as much as his entire body – he exited his study and walked down the stairs, registering that his house had never seemed so foreign. He felt like he was intruding on someone else's space. As though his home had been taken over by an unwelcomed other. Some entity that didn't want him here. Something, apparently, that was throwing a party for a long-dead boy.

"Happy birthday to you!"

When he got downstairs he was met with another surprise.

The newspapers. They were back.

Not new newspapers; these were the same printed articles he had torn, bunched up, thrown in garbage bags and lugged to his workshop only to have them vanish. And now they were here, still torn and bunched, but thrown all over the first level of his house. No, not all over, he quickly realized. This was a literal paper trail, leading toward the kitchen and into the living room. To the place where all the sounds were being made.

The singing started over.

"Happy birthday to you..."

Corbray stalled once again, his back to his front door, his front to the kitchen. He considered turning and fleeing and continuing to do so until this nightmare was left behind. But, if he fled, would it only be these intruders who would chase him? Or would The Fold be in pursuit of him as well, worrying that he was fleeing in order to divulge their secrets.

He turned to the front door, not to leave but to make sure that it was locked, which it was. He understood that he couldn't go anywhere. He had to settle this – whatever this was – now. Then find a way to reach Elareen and let her know he was not an issue. Let her know that any issue had been resolved. There was no running from this.

He could see a portion of the kitchen from where he stood. Just enough to note that the lights, which had previously been turned off, were now on. That the floor was littered with newspapers, bunched and balled.

He could hear the singing coming from beyond the entry to that room. And he was terrified.

"Happy birthday, dear Philip..."

He willed his feet to walk toward the choir, holding the letter opener in front of him the same way he had previously held the pistol he now desperately wished he had. A pistol that might be waiting for him in the hands of an intruder just beyond the entryway of the kitchen. A pistol that was likely meant to put a bullet in his brain from the moment it had been given to him. He pushed that thought from his mind as he walked through the doorway with the letter opener ahead of him. It shook violently in his unsteady hands. His entire body vibrated with fear.

When he saw what waited for him in the dining room, just beyond his kitchen, that fear turned to terror. His vibrating body began to tremor.

He dropped the letter opener, ran to the chopping block on the counter to his left, upgraded his weaponry to a butcher knife and pointed it toward the dining room table.

A table upon which sat a cake. It's candles – thirteen of them – long guttered out.

The cake, he could see, had **HAPPY ANNIVERSARY!** written obnoxiously upon it in blue icing on white frosting. The letters were hard to discern because of the melted candles. Wax and ash covered the top of the baked good from wicks fully burned through.

There was no one at the table. No one but Philip.

It was a picture of Philip Toles waiting there for Corbray. One of the pictures from the newspapers. Enlarged. Blown out. It was taped to a chair. The photo of the boy, its eyes, its mouth, had been cut out. It was this photograph Philip who had sat there as the candles burned into his cake, incapable of doing otherwise. Just like the dead boy he represented.

"Happy birthday to you..."

The singing had never ceased. And now Corbray could see why. He turned his attention to his right, to the television in his living room visible from the kitchen. From what he could tell, he was the only one here watching what was playing. That fact should have relaxed him, but it only tensed him further. He turned and looked around him, expecting someone to be at his back. Expecting many someones to leap out from many somewheres and turn this game into something serious. More serious than it already was.

When he was convinced this wouldn't happen, he turned back to the television. A television which should have been off. It played a video that should not have been playing on the screen.

It was a birthday party

It was a single shot, a scene playing repeatedly. A video of a young boy aged three years, based on the candles on the cake in front of him. He sat there smiling and clapping as he was serenaded. Clapping so excitedly that the wind from his hands nearly blew out the candles before he could do so purposefully. When he did get to blow out his candles, he got them all in one go, causing the room to break out in applause, some cheering and encouraging the boy as most continued to sing.

"Happy birthday, to you..."

The video replayed. It did so endlessly. Mr. Corbray had no idea what to make of it. How to rationalize this thing that was impossible. Illogical.

He wouldn't have believed the situation could get any stranger, not even if someone had told him to expect it to. But then he heard a sound behind him. One that was supposed to make him feel secure. It now filled him with ice cold dread.

"**This house is armed!**" the mechanical voice rang throughout the house.

His front door had been opened.

His front door, which he had made sure was locked when he came down the stairs, was now no longer secured.

He turned toward the sound, raised the knife in that direction. Thought, this time, about running and hiding and allowing the alarm, which was already counting down and sure to soon go off, to contact the police and bring them here.

He already knew whoever was doing this had his gun, though he didn't know how many of them there were. Or just what sort of brazen beasts might be walking into his house on this early morning.

Just as he was turning toward the back door to escape from whoever had broken in, he heard another sound. A telltale noise.

It was six rapid beeps. It was the same sound he made with his finger against the alarm keypad when he entered or exited the house.

It was the sound of someone inputting a password.

No fucking chance, he thought. *No damn way they'll guess my code.* He had barely finished the thought when he heard the word,

"Disarmed!"

"Oh..." Mr. Corbray said, and was frozen to the spot by a mix of fear and morbid curiosity.

Moments after the alarm had been deactivated, the singing behind him stopped. The house was filled with the sort of silence that consumes.

Silence. Except for footsteps. Walking toward him.

Silence. Except for the sound of a person entering the doorway to the kitchen and stopping there. Standing there.

Someone impossible. Someone illogical.

It was silent, except for when that person who was standing there cleared his throat.

The person standing in the entryway wore a wet forest green rain slicker, black boots, black pants. He had one hand behind his back while he used the other to adjust the red baseball cap on his head. Not once did he take his eyes away from Morris Corbray, who was in the middle of the kitchen still holding an unsteady knife in a tremulous hand.

The boy staring from the doorway spoke.

"Mr. Corbray?" Philip Toles said to the former guidance counsellor. His voice was friendly, though his face bore no expression. "Am I late for the party?"

****

Run!

Run! Run! Run! Run! Run! Run! Run!

That word, that urge, was the center of all his thoughts.

Mr. Corbray dropped the knife. Turned to flee the moment the ghost from his past asked him the question. He was eager to leave this party. This gathering of grief.

He dashed to the back exit. Zipped through the kitchen and was there in moments. Unfortunately for him, for a few seconds, he forgot how the back door functioned. A few seconds that felt like each of them might be his last.

He struggled with the handle, the door not moving. He eventually remembered to push down the button which would unlock it. The door began to slide as he heard slow footsteps approaching behind him.

"Mr. Corbray? Why are you in such a rush to leave?" Philip asked, sounding genuinely perplexed.

Run! Run! Run! Run!

One door solved, he opened the screen door next, nearly ripping through it. Opened the exterior door after that. Cursed the fact that there were so many fucking doors.

RUN!

He ran. More accurately, he attempted to run. He took a long and powerful stride onto his back deck. He felt fresh air. *Freedom! Escape!*

Run! Run! Run! Ru–

He felt something smash against the side of his head. Felt pain. Then he felt the wooden deck as he fell.

After that, he felt nothing.

FOURTEEN.

That was the number of times the video reel had replayed itself.

It was not the same recording of the birthday party, and he was not in his living room.

Morris Corbray was in his workshop. He was viewing this new video from a laptop which had been set up on a workbench to his right. He was wearing his shirt but was naked from the waist down. Testicles slick with nervous sweat were plastered to the wooden chair he was strapped to. His limbs were zip tied at his wrists and ankles to the limbs of the chair. Where he wasn't tied he was taped.

Corbray's torso was duct taped – from just below his nipples to just above his bellybutton – tightly, in several rounds, to the back of the chair. The chair itself, each leg, was designed in such a way that had allowed it to be bolted to the floor. Mr. Corbray had absolutely nowhere to go. Nothing to do but pay attention to the video playing on the bench beside him.

He didn't have to watch it. There was nothing physically forcing him to look in that direction. All he had to do was turn his head and look away to avoid it. But that would mean looking at the newspapers on the wall. The pictures. The reminders.

Much like his bedroom on the day he had returned from his vacation – a day that felt like a year ago now – the walls of his workshop were plastered with newspapers. These newspapers were accompanied by photos that had been enlarged and made into posters.

There were leaflets on the wall as well, literature that had been distributed to the community after Philip had died. Documents related to holding the school responsible, to keeping children out of the hands of pedophiles. Included among these were several copies of the same leaflet Corbray had found on his car the morning after leaving his daughter's house. Also included among these were many photos of a particular pedophile.

Pictures of Mr. Morris Corbray, the former guidance counsellor, the current youth minister, were all over the walls.

Photos of him in the act of pedophilia, pederasty, child exploitation, and rape. Pictures he himself had taken over the course of nearly two decades. Images he had placed in a bag beneath the floor of this very workshop. In a place he had thought would be safe even if the police had one day found reason to search his property. Yet the bag had been found, and its contents were all over the walls.

Its contents were also playing on the video which had now looped for the fifteenth time for Mr. Corbray's viewing and listening pleasure.

It was a compilation film displaying his depravities. Each time it restarted, it wasn't the children he had violated that he thought of, despite seeing them there on the computer screen. What he thought of was the fact that he felt as though *he* had been violated. His privacy eliminated over the last week, perhaps longer.

In the reel, interspersed amongst the filthy pictures, the illegal videos, the proof of his perversions, were recordings of him doing mundane things. Of him in his current house walking around, putting food and water in Jar Jar's bowls. There was a short clip of him at his new alarm system's keypad, clearly punching in the code. Him leaving and entering the upstairs bathroom or his bedroom. General surveillance of his home from top to bottom.

One of the clips in this ever-running reel was of a figure, a boy in a red cap and green rain jacket, walking around his living room, pausing to stop and give Jar Jar a treat as the dog followed the stranger around the house amicably. It was obvious now how he had been able to do all he had done, including stealing the dog, without Jar Jar making a fuss.

When Corbray had first seen this collection of images and recordings, he had waited, watched desperately, hoping not to see a video of them slaughtering his dog in some tribalistic measure of revenge. He was terrified that his pet and best friend would pay the price for his sins.

But that video never came. Though so many others did.

There was a brief clip of the boy in the red cap walking into Corbray's study while he slept. Standing over him, hovering over the gun, picking up the pistol. It cut to the next scene abruptly. Each time Corbray saw that clip of the boy lurking over him and his pistol, he understood how close he had been to death.

But how close had he been to someone already dead?

When he had woken up, bound, seeing this video playing on the workbench beside him, he had felt confident that, though he was in trouble, he wasn't dealing with something supernatural. Not some ghost which had been sneaking around his house and following him wherever he went, but a real person, or people, toying with his life for who knows how long. Ramping up their games for this, the big anniversary. Philip's date of birth. The day he had been found dead.

He had been convinced it couldn't be some phantom until the footage of the boy in his study holding the gun. Until he saw with his own two eyes someone he was more than certain he had murdered standing in front of him at his desk. Saw him turn and look directly into the camera for the first time.

And there it had been, the face of Philip Toles. Not pasted on a piece of paper, but moving, visually recorded walking around Morris Corbray's home.

He didn't know what to make of it. Either the footage was doctored, ghosts were real, or he was losing his mind.

He told himself that the footage was doctored. That it was an impersonator who had startled him in his kitchen and in the church's basement. He tried to convince himself that this was part of the game someone – whoever this person was – had been playing all this time.

But the child in the video was clearly Philip Toles. A dead boy. Walking.

Corbray had seen him, heard him. And, from the pain in Corbray's head where he had been hit, and his side where he had landed, it was possible he had felt Philip's touch as well.

Philip had come back from the past, from the beyond, to try him for his crimes. The trial Corbray had avoided by sending Kathleen Jeffreys to prison. He had a feeling Philip would not be as lenient as the judge who had presided over Kathleen's case had been.

He tried to stop himself from thinking in those terms. From thinking this was Philip. He couldn't truly believe that the boy had somehow come back to haunt him, could he? It was crazy, the idea of ghosts. Absolutely foolish. Yet he was sure he had seen a boy who looked just like the one in the photos all around him. A boy who had led him into this trap. The same student whom he had murdered thirteen years ago. A child, Corbray saw as he recoiled into the chair he was strapped to, who had just walked into the workshop.

****

Corbray had never felt a fear as intense as this. A spurt of urine sprayed from his exposed penis, leaving a wet line on the dusty flooring of the shed. A spurt, then dribbles, resulting in the seat beneath him suddenly turning wet and warm as his bladder released without him instructing it to.

He felt like a vulnerable toddler. And, like a vulnerable toddler, Morris Corbray began to blubber. He didn't just cry, he bawled, screamed, begged for the dead boy to stop walking toward him. To leave him alone.

"I'm sorry. Philip, please! *Please*, you know how I felt about you. I loved you... I *love* you! I just didn't want to lose you, so I did what I thought was best. But I know now that I was wrong and I'm sorry. I'm so sorry."

But Philip only continued to walk toward him. Corbray could see now that, inside the green rain slicker, Philip wore an orange shirt with white stripes. The same shirt he had been wearing in his Picture Day picture. And it wasn't just any red hat he wore, it was the same bloodred colour with the same bloodred maple leaf in the center of it. He had never seen anyone but Philip wear this specific special edition Toronto Blue Jays cap.

Just like he used to dress, he noted grimly.

The boy's hands were behind his back, and Corbray was wracked with a dread so strong that his body began to shudder.

He hung his head. In fear. In shame. All manner of liquid – tears, snot, saliva – leaked from his face onto his chest, his lap. He pleaded more. Mumbling, begging, his words a watery wave, directionless as they seeped from his sopping wet mouth. A stream of indecipherable sounds that translated to 'Please don't kill me'. Noises that could be interpreted as 'Even though I violated you and murdered you and now you're back to bring me justice, I hope you can find it in your heart to think that this is enough. I hope you can take into consideration that I am sitting in my own piss, and I am shamed.' These were the things he hoped to convey as he sat and wetly whined.

The boy stopped a few feet in front of him. Only stood there and watched him. Glaring. Not responding to anything Corbray said.

Those same blue eyes, the same mouth, though not the way he remembered it. Not as it had been thirteen years ago, smiling, always asking questions. Now it was set in a grim line. A judgmental expression.

Morris Corbray was not ready to be judged. Not with all of his sins laid out so blatantly around him.

"Please," he said once more, this time clearly. "I'm so sorry for what I did, Philip. But you have to understand that I thought I *had* to. You were making a mistake! A *mistake*! You were going to throw away both our lives for that *woman!*"

The boy only stared, his hands still behind his back. Beneath the brim of his cap his face looked like damnation.

"Please! Just... Let me see your hands... Let me see them and you can put whatever that is down, and we can talk. We can *talk*! I can make it up to you. I have..." he was going to say money. But what was money to a vengeful spirit? "...I have..." he couldn't think of a single thing he could give to this boy that would make up for what he had taken away. "...I'm sorry!" is what he settled upon, feebly.

Head hung, Corbray continued to cry. These were tears of regret, though not of guilt. Not of true remorse. These were tears that, when streaking down his face, would have spelled out upon his skin a message such as:

'I wish I hadn't gotten caught'.

Or, perhaps:

'I should have killed you better.'

He was hoping the boy wouldn't be able to read those tears for what they were.

Corbray was preparing to release another volley of pleas when he heard the sound of the workshop door opening again. A second person was entering the outbuilding.

For a moment there was hope. The dream of a potential rescue.

That dream was short-lived.

What he experienced, when this second person was fully through the door, was disappointment. The loss of hope. A nightmare exacerbated.

There was disappointment because he should have realized who it was this entire time. There was the loss of hope because there was no chance this person would forgive him.

Each day of the thirteen years that had passed since Philip's death was evident in the lines and wrinkles on the face which was looking down at Morris Corbray. The years had been harsh. But despite those harsh years, this person carried a twisted sort of energy. Upon that face was a smile that looked like joyful cruelty. The sort of cruelty that fueled. That kept people like this young.

Corbray's exacerbated nightmare had a name:

"Solomon! M-Mr. Toles!"

He was staring at the haggard yet happy looking face of the grandfather of Philip Toles. Beneath a cream-coloured Panama hat, he saw a face like a missing puzzle piece.

Looking at it now caused everything to fall into place. Caused Corbray to see the entire picture. Suddenly it all made sense.

He looked to the boy wearing the red hat. Watched the old man walk toward him.

"The baby…" Mr. Corbray whispered, realization hitting him like the rays of a dawning sun. "My God, the baby…"

"You did good, kid. Real good," Solomon Toles said as he walked over to the boy. With a hand covered in a second skin of purple latex, he removed the red cap from the boy's head. Ruffled his hair.

Hair that was more strawberry blonde than the brown Corbray remembered. Hair that reminded him of that which had belonged to the now-deceased Kathleen Jeffreys.

The boy smiled, laughed. Said,

"Thanks, Big Pop!" He removed one of his hands from behind his back. To Corbray's dismay, he saw that it was covered by a purple latex glove much like Solomon's. With that gloved hand, he brushed his too-light hair from his too-broad forehead.

The eyes, the lips, the nose, all the same. But the differences were clear now. He should have seen it all along.

"Mr. Corbray," Solomon 'Big Pop' Toles said, almost conversationally, "I would like for you to meet my great-grandson. Philip Toles, the second."

"FIFTEEN years ago, my wife passed away," Solomon Toles said as he stood in front of a bound and frightened Morris Corbray. "Around that same time, you divorced your wife. Have I got that right? Anyway, they called it a short battle with cancer, but it felt like a long war to me. One we were bound to lose from the start. But it gave us time, bad as it was. It gave us time to make sure there were no regrets, and nothing left unsaid. In the end, it was ugly and painful, but at least I knew she had peace of mind. The only thing she asked of me was to look after Philip. Said she didn't trust our daughter-in-law to raise him right without our boy around to help. As you know, our son is dead, also of cancer, and Philip was all we had of him. I swore on my soul I would protect my grandson. And I did my best to, I think. Though some nights it's hard to accept that, seeing how things turned out.

"But what was I to do? I couldn't leave my business and move. His mom wouldn't agree to move out to me, so I did my best to see him in the summer and on holidays. I did my best to give him a good male influence. I thought I was doing okay, you know. I wasn't dad of the year with my own son – I was definitely a better grandpa than a father – but I tried. I still look at that picture of us fishing, and I wonder what went wrong. Then I remember that what went wrong was you, and people like you,"

Solomon had been speaking for quite some time.

Venting.

"No! It was Jeffreys! She was the one who started it. I..."

Solomon, the moment Corbray decided to interrupt him, removed a hook from the right pocket of his brown overcoat. A fist-sized hook which dangled from the end of a chain. He didn't say anything, only let it hang by his side.

Corbray began to hyperventilate as he watched the hook swaying there. Eventually, with a calmness of body that contradicted the violence in his eyes, Solomon Toles asked,

"May I continue?"

Corbray, in his tremulous terror, seemed to nod half a hundred times in the matter of a second, his head a hummingbird's wing.

"I could accept tragedy," Solomon continued, "My life's been full of them. My son, diagnosed with terminal cancer in his twenties. Shitty luck. What can you do? My wife, cancer as well. Twice in the same family within a decade? It's terrible, but that does happen. When I was a teenager, my brother got himself killed working in the factories down in Old Coal Town. Back before the city closed them down and turned that place into a slum. You were living in Saturn for that, right?"

Corbray was still nodding, trying to focus on Solomon's words, but he was too distracted by the dull-looking hook hanging from the man's gloved fist. Solomon continued,

"With my brother it was wrong place, wrong time. With my wife and son, it was bad luck, bad circumstances. Things happen sometimes. Even terrible things. You gotta accept it and move on. So, if something had *happened* to Philip, I would have been able to accept it. But suicide? I never, ever, ever, ever, ever, not for *one* single moment believed it was possible. That may have just been a grandfather thinking the best of his pup, but I didn't buy it. To be fair, I had a hard time buying that he was sleeping with a teacher, but I could accept that. Philip was curious and impressionable like his grandpa was, like most lads are. But he was full of life, and he would never have put that life out on his own. I knew that. *Knew it*. Knew it to my core.

"But it wasn't until I received a letter from Kathleen Jeffreys, the last person I expected to be contacted by, that I understood the truth. And when I say she was the last person I expected to be contacted by, I mean the *very* last. She had been dead for nearly seven years when the letter was delivered. Her sister sent it long after receiving that wretched woman's belongings from the prison and not going through them for some time.

"At first, I thought it was a joke and I wasn't going to pay it any mind. Things were improving for me by that time. That took a while though, for things to improve, I mean. At first things only seemed to get worse and worse. Philip's mom ditched me not long after the funeral. Left me to foot the bill for the kid's headstone and coffin. Those things are Goddamn expensive, I'll tell ya. She left me with a lot of... issues to take care of..." He said this last sentence contemplatively, as though remembering everything he had gone through for the first time in years.

"But I handled it... Long story short, the situation with Philip's mom led to me meeting someone. A lawyer, actually. Said she could help me get Philip's son. You remember when we talked about me adopting him, you little fucking rat?" After saying this to Corbray, the old man paused to look at his great-grandson. "Excuse my language, kid."

Philip II let out a little giggle as though he had been let in on an inside joke. Solomon went on.

"You remember sitting in front of me and consoling me about my boy after knowing what you knew and doing what you did?" He sounded angrier, but he didn't sound any different at the same time. His voice was controlled rage, and Mr. Corbray was sure the hook the man held was bound to enter him at any moment. But Solomon made no violent movement with his body. Only stood. Only talked.

"The lawyer, my partner, she helped me get Philip's boy. It was a struggle and it took a few years, but I eventually adopted PJ out of the foster system. But not before he had been left with a lot of... issues as well. By people like you. Just like I told you I was worried about. Remember that, you fucking rat? Yeah, you remember. But I handled that as well." He again looked at his great-grandson as he said that last sentence. They locked eyes lovingly. Philip II smiled, as did his Big Pop. But something in their eyes seemed to be tainted. Laced with venom. Solomon turned his venom-laced eyes back to Corbray.

"I was content with just raising my great-grandson right, and not worrying about the past so much. Then I got the letter. And the more I looked into what the Jeffreys woman said, the more I realized that there were lessons I needed to teach young PJ. Especially after all he had been through. Lessons that he couldn't learn from his schoolbooks. And while I taught him everything he knows, I kept in mind that you and I were long overdue to have another sit-down. When I found out about your retirement, I figured we would have plenty of free time to do some reminiscing. It's been nearly thirteen years since we sat and chatted. You have any idea how much catching up we have to do, Mr. Corbray?"

"No. I... It's a mistake. She... ahhhhhh... she... uhh... What did she say?" Nervous gibberish. Even with the evidence all around him, he wouldn't – couldn't – bring himself to acknowledge what he had done.

"What do you think she said?" Rhetorical. Literal. There was no answer either way. Corbray was not willing to say it out loud.

After a few moments of silence, Solomon Toles walked behind the chair Mr. Corbray was strapped to. Philip II stood with his hands still behind his back while watching the two men. His eyes were hungry. He was learning from his great-grandfather even then, curious to see what he would do with that hook.

Fear, extreme fear, makes musicians of us all.

A person might never know they could be a songster until the moment they are certain they are going to die.

Slowly. Painfully.

Morris Corbray was humming deeply, breathing loudly, filling the workshop with the music of his soul. Soon there would be high notes, pitches and tones he never would have thought himself capable of creating.

Philip II watched eagerly as his Big Pop plunged the hook into Mr. Corbray's chest, right below the collarbone, anchoring it in there. Deep.

This inspired the first high note.

Solomon yanked back on the chain. The hook dug in beneath Mr. Corbray's collarbone, threatening to pull it away from the rest of his body. His body that was strapped and taped to the chair. The chair which was bolted to the floor. His clavicle was far more likely to be wrenched free of him before he would be free of his bonds.

He displayed so much vocal range as his shirt went from grey to red in seconds.

Philip II smiled. Took note.

When the screams diminished to whispers, Solomon Toles asked, again, perhaps more clearly this time,

"What do you think her letter said, Mr. Corbray?"

"That I... That I was with him..."

Solomon yanked back on the chain. High pitched notes again.

Mr. Corbray was a fish caught, waiting to see if he would be freed or filleted. He decided, through red agony, that if he was to make it out of here alive, he had better tell the truth.

"The letter said that I took advantage of your grandson! And that... and that I had a role in his death!" He didn't want to admit to murder. They could blame him for Philip's state of mind, blame him for the suicide as they had blamed Kathleen, but he could still have a life after several years in prison so long as he didn't admit to murder. This was his brightest hope at the moment. Imprisonment. As well as a lenient provincial judge.

The hook twisted in his chest. More music from his mouth.

"Had a role?" Solomon asked. "You hear that, PJ?"

"I heard it, Big Pop! What do you think he means?"

"I don't know. Maybe you ought to ask him."

The boy with Philip's face grinned at Mr. Corbray as he finally moved. He had been standing at ease with his hands behind his back. Now he stood straight, removed his gloved hands from behind him. Revealed an extremely sharp-looking fillet knife.

The boy fell to his knees in front of Mr. Corbray, who might have relished the sight of this if not for the hook in his chest. And now the blade of a knife slicing rapidly and ruthlessly between the toes of his right foot, cutting through the tender skin there.

More sounds he never thought he could be capable of making escaped him. Amongst them were the only three words that mattered:

"I killed him!" he cried. "I killed Philip! Please! Stop! I admit it. I..." the rest was unintelligible.

Philip II had started on the left foot, not slicing this time but sawing between the toes, back and forth, up and down.

"Pleeeeeeeeeasssssssssssssse!" Mr. Corbray begged, his voice like a whistling kettle.

"PJ! Hey! Wait a second," Mr. Corbray heard Solomon say to the son of his son's son. The boy stopped sawing and turned to his great-grandfather. Corbray thought for a moment that Solomon was going to tell his descendant to stop. Prayed that this would be so. But when the elder Toles continued to speak, Corbray understood that all was lost.

"You can go ahead, kid. But remember, go slowly. We really want him to appreciate your work."

The man was mad, the boy a madman's tool.

And a sharp one.

Anxiety. Fear. Panic. The need to flee caused his body to react despite being bound to the spot. All of his adrenaline threatened to burst from him. He shuddered and shook with great violence, his heart thundering as he did so. He wondered if he might not simply shake to death just now. Believed, in this moment, that he might be at risk of being literally scared to death.

Because the boy had a smile on his face and a knife in his hand, and both the knife and the smile were now aimed at Morris Corbray's exposed genitals.

He went to cry out again, but at that moment Philip II stopped. Looked carefully at him as if reconsidering what he had clearly been trained to do. Mr. Corbray took this to be a positive sign.

"Thank you! Thank you... You don't need to do th—"

"Big Pop, you forgot the gag," Philip II said, looking over Corbray's shoulder at his great-grandfather. "He's never gonna shut up if you don't use it. That's like the first thing you taught me." Then he giggled.

Mr. Corbray had never heard such evil noise.

"Well done, PJ. Your Pop got caught up in the moment."

The old man walked around from behind Corbray, twisting and wrenching and yanking the hook from the minister's chest before doing so. There was screaming. Begging. All ignored.

Solomon wiped the hook clean with a rag before placing the weapon back in his right pocket. Then he removed from his left pocket a black ball gag with a leather metal-studded strap. Something Morris had seen in kink stores in the past. Something he had only experimented with on others prior to now. An object he was not eager to have placed into his mouth at the moment. But when he went to protest, to move his head away from the approaching gag in the old man's hands, he felt the tip of the boy's knife at the far too thin and tender skin of his scrotum. He looked from the old man's cold green eyes to the crazed and excited blue gems inside the head of this boy who looked like a demented version of the father he never knew. A version of the Philip who never grew beyond this boy's age.

This was Philip, but twisted.

This was Philip. Corrupted.

Resigned, he opened his mouth, allowing the gag to be shoved in. There was blood from Solomon's hands – from Morris Corbray's chest – on the ball gag. The coppery taste of it flooded his mouth. Then the straps were tightened around the back of his head and neck. He hoped that if he cooperated they might have mercy on him. He hoped...

His hope lasted only until he felt the knife go in, pinning his favourite part of him to the seat beneath. He tried to bellow but the gag distorted the sound.

"Easy, kid. Let him appreciate it... And remember, PJ. Don't chop, slice. Mr. Corbray here is the sort of fella who has to learn by the layer. And slowly."

"Sorry, Big Pop. This time I got caught up in the moment." They both chuckled at that. Then the boy removed the knife that was pinning Mr. Corbray's penis to the seat beneath it. Changing his tactic, heeding his great-grandfather's advice, he slowly, ever so slowly, began to slice. Began to skin.

Morris Corbray produced muffled yet majestic noise. More music to the ears of the two Toles. A hymn being hummed. A song no God would answer.

Big Pop smiled while PJ continued cutting. He ripped one of the newspapers from the wall and began to read out loud all that had been done to corrupt and kill his grandson.

"**S**IXTEEN was how old I was when I lost my virginity. Set me on a path to have a son at a pretty young age myself. Philip's dad had him at a respectable age, in his mid-twenties. But you knew all this, considering you were his counsellor and all. My own history's why I could rationalize him being with that teacher, I suppose. Most boys that age would do it because they think it's the cool thing to do. And people like her prey on that. And people like *you* feed on what's left over. Philip didn't even know he was broken but you just kept on chipping away, eh?"

At this point, Morris Corbray barely understood what was going on. The ball gag had been removed from his mouth, largely because he was no longer capable of screaming, tongueless and lipless as he was. He mainly whimpered. Cried. Whimpered. Prayed for death. But Death wouldn't answer.

Solomon, along with Philip's spawn, fed Mr. Corbray. He thought it was mostly applesauce that they took turns spooning into his mouth, but everything tasted like blood and pain. They gave him water that made him feel as though he were drinking cups full of pennies.

All of this so they could keep him alive. Keep him alive to kill him slowly.

The Corruption of Philip Toles

The entire time, all throughout his agony, Solomon Toles, locksmith turned vigilante, talked at him about the reason he was sitting in this chair, as if the photos and the videos and the anguish didn't spell it out clearly enough for the former guidance counsellor, recent retiree.

From time to time, the boy would speak as well, raving like his great-grandfather, clearly a fast learner and a smart child.

"Men like you make bad people. To stop making bad people, we have to stop bad people like you," Philip II had said matter-of-factly on one of the many occasions when Mr. Corbray had mumbled some combination or variation of the words "You don't have to do this." Back when he had been capable of saying such a sentence.

This was after the boy had extracted flesh, removed skin, cut the man to the bone.

"It's all about stopping the cycle of evil and predation," the child had added. "*You* said that in an interview once. After you killed my dad. I read it in the newspapers. I read a lot of things you said. It used to make me confused because I didn't understand how you could say so many good things but be such a bad man. But Big Pop explained it. He said people like you are 'full of shit.' I guess that's what we're gonna find out." Then he had gone back to cutting. Expertly ensuring the man didn't bleed out. His small hands like those of a masterful surgeon.

Corbray didn't know how long he had been locked inside of his workshop. He recalled, in this red haze, that Solomon had tortured the name of his main contact at the church out of him before they had cut out his tongue. They had called Deacon James, forcing Minister Corbray to speak to the man of God while a knife was beneath his testicles, its tip at his anus. Corbray had let the Deacon know that he would not be in attendance for Friday's youth group. Minister Corbray still wasn't feeling very well, it seemed.

Deacon James had responded kindly, telling him to take it easy. Saying that they would see him next Wednesday. And that he would be there to help Minister Corbray during this transition until he was fully ready for the role.

Deacon James had wished him the best. Corbray had fought against the urge to beg for help. He had known that the moment he begged for help, he would die. And he had still been hopeful, maybe, by some miracle, that he would be saved. That he could find his way out of this as he had with every other situation that had seemed to be an impediment to him before.

That hope now seemed like a foolish thing. He should have cried for help, he understood upon reflection. But not because he thought Deacon James would have been able to save him, but because, at this point, he would rather be dead. All he had done was ensure that Solomon and his great-grandson had nearly an entire week to prolong his torture before people would begin to wonder where he was.

He'd stopped counting the number of times the video had replayed on the laptop after over two hundred reruns. He felt as though that might have been over two hundred reruns ago.

Sometimes, he still thought he had his fingers. They would itch and tingle even beneath all the pain. During those times, he would still go to flex them, wiggle them around. Then a fresh burst of pain would rip through him, a reminder that the boy and the old man had taken turns using Mr. Corbray's own pruning shears to lop off his digits.

In one corner of the shed, they'd been hanging and drying the parts of him they had removed. Like jerky.

At this point, death seemed as though it might be as pleasant as his last vacation had been.

He tried not to think about that. Thinking of pleasure and listening to the sex sounds that still played from the laptop beside him only made him hurt down there even more than he constantly had since the boy had started in on him with the fillet knife.

Like his fingers, he sometimes felt as though *that* was still there, too.

He couldn't always distinguish when he was asleep from when he was awake. His nightmares were nearly just as painful as his waking woe. There was one occasion, though, when he had thought he was having a pleasant dream. The only happy moment he'd had while strapped inside of that shed.

Jar Jar had walked into the workshop. Had Corbray still been able to pronounce the dog's name, he would have called out to him. Cried out for joy. Would have asked his dog to go get help.

The happy moment had been short-lived. Because the dog had been followed in by Solomon and Philip Toles II.

Mr. Corbray tried to beg them away, but his voice had been a series of wet smacking sounds. And it had hurt for him to make those noises.

He remembered Jar Jar in the video taking treats from Philip II. Saw that the dog was willingly walking alongside Corbray's two torturers.

"You hungry, little guy?" Corbray heard the boy ask. And before he knew what was going on, Philip II had turned his blade to Corbray again. Was digging and turning and tearing something out of his left forearm. A chunk. A portion. One of many they had taken from him so far that would equate to their pound of flesh. Several pounds, it felt like.

Haven't they had enough retribution yet? he wondered, when his mind wasn't all pain.

His eyes hazy with agony, he watched as Philip II walked over to the corner of the workshop. He stuck the piece of Corbray he had just removed onto one of many small hooks hanging from a taut wire that stretched between two walls. From another hook on that wire, he took one of the previously hung and dried portions of the retired guidance counsellor and offered it to Jar Jar.

To Corbray's dismay and revulsion, he saw that his best friend had happily accepted the snack, eating the partially dried slice of ear directly from the young boy's hand. Licking his master's blood from Philip II's fingers.

Traitor, Corbray thought at the dog. Then he passed out from two different kinds of pain.

Passed out to find himself in a lucid nightmare.

He was at the doorway of Foster's Family Restaurant.

He went to open the door and saw that the handle was different than he remembered. Ornate. Instead of the standard set of vertical pull bars he was accustomed to, there was only a single handle. And it was a knob. One shaped like the number 8 tipped sideways. Six red gems bejeweled it – three in one portion of the '8' and three in the other. It gleamed like polished jet stone against the wood it was embedded into.

He turned the knob and opened the door, feeling an unpleasant energy course from his hand throughout his body. He looked in expecting to see the restaurant he had so loved to frequent. What he saw instead was a road.

A road that seemed to be made of black ice with veins of bright blues and reds running throughout it. The sky around The Road was the Cosmos. On either side of it there was nothing but rising and billowing fog. Electric blue.

On The Road was his usual table.

At that table was the unusual waitress.

The Red Lady.

The Corruption of Philip Toles

She was still naked and full of holes. She carried with Her a number of trays, balancing them with Her arms and hands and chin like only a trained waitress can.

On the trays were pieces of Philip Toles, Mr. Corbray saw from the doorway as he looked into the restaurant. As he looked out into Infinity. She had carried the dead boy there in separated parts.

The Red Waitress placed Philip on the table, treating each plate containing a part of him like a puzzle.

A head, torso, legs. Connecting pieces. Rebuilding him.

He almost looks whole again, Mr. Corbray thought. And, in the dream, he cried tears that turned into a waterfall. A waterfall which flowed into the restaurant, down The Road, formed a river. He wept and watched as this river gushed around the feet of the waitress.

The water, his tears, began to boil.

She turned to look at Mr. Corbray as She lifted Philip's head – his red hat back on it – from one of the plates, turning it, making sure it was facing Mr. Corbray's direction when she connected it to his torso. He now looked complete as he lay on the table on his side.

Philip opened eyes which were unnaturally blue. Like all the fog around him.

He blinked. Blinked again. Then stared unblinkingly at his old guidance counsellor, his predator and murderer. He somehow still had the white noose he had been hung with wrapped around his neck. The rope pooled around his body on the table. She stood beside him as he lay there, both looking at Mr. Corbray.

The Red Lady and The Boy With The Hangman's Noose said something that was soundless. Something in unison.

Mr. Corbray struggled to hear them. Couldn't.

He watched them mouth words. Tried to read their lips. Couldn't.

They repeated themselves several more times as he observed their mouths closely and intently, reading individual words here and there until he formed the sentence. Understood what they were saying. And knew he should have understood it all along.

It was the same thing he'd been told each time he had left Foster's Family Restaurant. And it was the last thing he wanted to be told now as he looked in and out and at oblivion.

"We hope to see you soon!"

Then The Road tilted to the left, tilted drastically, and Mr. Corbray felt as though he were rolling off of it, into a cold Blue Abyss.

He woke up slanted in his chair. Leaning to the left.

Each time he woke from one of these nightmares it was to some new torture. Sometimes that torture would simply be the sound of the workshop door opening. A sound that had at first given Mr. Corbray some hope.

Maybe my daughter has come check on me.

Maybe Riley told them about the secret game we played when I was in his bed, and his dad has come here to kick my ass.

Corbray would happily face that over this.

Maybe it would be a good Samaritan, some saviour at the workshop door who had heard his screams before he had lost his lips and tongue.

But it never was.

It was always the grandfather, the boy.

His reckoning. His punishment.

Sometimes, it was only one of them. Sometimes, as he was witnessing currently, it was both.

Solomon Toles and Philip Toles II walked into the shed. Mr. Corbray immediately began to attempt to reason with them.

"I think he's trying to talk, Big Pop."

"Plllesssshhhhdunnnnt. Saaawweeeeee."

Mr. Corbray was begging again.

Solomon smiled at the bound man. One would think he was about to discuss bygone remembrances with an old friend. His watery eyes had a lunatic quality to them, a hint of which Corbray had first seen in the courtroom when he had so naively believed he was never going to face the consequences for what he had done. In Solomon's eyes now, Corbray saw the same mad desperation the man had shown when they had sat for lunch. Except what had been a glimmer of madness then was now a glaring glow. Full blown lunacy. And judging from the eyes of Philip II, this madness had made its way down through the generations.

Solomon grabbed an item from the sprawling worktable to Corbray's left.

He produced a clothing iron. It was steaming hot.

Corbray had no memory of them putting it there. Plugging it in.

Solomon's smile widened. Then he spoke. Not to Mr. Corbray, but to his grandson.

"Hurry up and get started, PJ. I've got a roast in the oven, and I don't want us to be late for lunch."

The boy nodded.

Has he blinked in all this time? Corbray wondered about Philip II. He thought not. It was the last thought he had before immediate pain became his world once again. But before that pain, before the boy went to work, he said something he had said several times prior. Some sort of mantra between the two family members in the workshop. As Philip II knelt in front of Corbray with a hacksaw in his hand, he said,

"For the Good Kids..."

"...And for the kids who never got the chance to be," his grandfather concluded, as he always did.

The hacksaw touched Mr. Corbray's skin at his ankle, then ripped through it as the serrated blade made its way to bone, one back and forth motion at a time.

He let out the first of ten thousand muffled, anguished groans during this session, each of which would fall upon uncaring ears.

The boy and the old man – A Man of Unspeakable Cruelty – were laughing at him, his misery their comedy, his torture their theatre. He gritted his teeth, which only filtered his moans. The agony was beyond anything he could have ever imagined.

A century later, as he whimpered and moaned, he felt his Achilles tendon severed as Philip II completed the barbarous amputation. He was begging for death at this point, eyes closed, mouth drooling. He had nearly passed out when he registered a hissing sound, almost like the sizzling of a cold piece of meat on a hot skillet.

Bacon. It smells like bacon. Then the pain worsened. The fullness of it causing him to open his eyes.

His leg – now missing a foot – had been cauterized by Solomon's steam iron.

"Good work, kid," Corbray heard the old man say, though he now sounded miles away. Unconsciousness was approaching, promising to take him again. But not before he heard Solomon speak once more.

"Let's take a break. It's time for lunch."

He watched through bleary eyes as great-grandfather and great-grandson left the shed, talking conversationally as though they hadn't been torturing a man for days.

He began to fade. But before he did so, he couldn't help but look at the many pictures among the newspapers on the walls. Images that illustrated the worst mistake of his life.

Photos that had made the front-page news, once upon a time. Pictures of a boy most had forgotten, but two had not.

Morris Corbray was haunted, taunted, teased, by the images that stared back at him, seeming to approve of his current situation.

Everywhere, all around him, he saw the smiling face of Philip Toles.

THANKS FOR READING!

I'm writing this Thank You portion of the book a few days removed from news of the Chicago Blackhawks/National Hockey League sexual assault scandal hitting the fan. Some of the coaches and executives responsible are now being held accountable a decade after the complaints of a male player and sexual assault victim had been ignored. His predator, a thing named Brad Aldrich, was subsequently allowed to roam free and sexually assault others, including a high school student. He eventually received nine months in jail for the assault of that child.

This sort of thing happens all the time. The signs and sometimes the outright cries for help are often there, but people are too uncomfortable to tackle them. Or too eager to silence victims for their own gains. In the above case, the Stanley Cup was more important than the mental health of an abused player and the future victimization of others. Children and vulnerable people continue to suffer, and so many people just don't seem to mind that. I've heard this sort of story a thousand times, as, I presume, you have, too.

It's that sort of story that motivated me to write The Corruption of Philip Toles. I liked the idea of having an ending where the pedophile doesn't get away with it. And doesn't receive a slap on the wrist after being discovered. I imagine this story wasn't comfortable to read. It wasn't comfortable for me to write, but I hope there was something in it that resonated with you.

The Corruption of Philip Toles was originally supposed to be part of my debut anthology, 'How To Make A Monster: The Loveliest Shade of Red'. I thought of it in February of 2017, but couldn't quite figure out how I wanted to tell the story in time to add it to the collection. It wasn't until February of 2021 that I started working on it again, completing the story quickly after that.

Despite the years between this novel and How To Make A Monster, The Corruption of Philip Toles is still very much connected to many of the stories in that anthology. So, if you're curious about Saturn City, Foster's Family Restaurant, and The Red Lady, you might want to check out How To Make A Monster. And if you're interested in reading more about The Fold – the organization that employs Elareen, The Beast in the Night – my debut novel, 'Bug Spray: A Tale of Madness' touches on The Fold in a bit more detail. You don't have to read these stories in any specific order, they are all meant to build upon each other in a stand-alone sort of way

As for the acknowledgements, I'd like to shout out the usual suspects, starting with Courtney Swank, who reads and supports everything I write. She is the person who puts all my words and wild ideas into book form. I will always be thankful for that.

A big thank you to Rosco Nischler, who is one of the best cover creators around. He also did the interior art for this book. As usual, he improved every idea I suggested to him.

And to my brother, Fred, who I dedicate everything to.

Also, a huge thank you to everyone who read this book (even the people who aren't reading this particular part of it) and my previous work. Your support has changed my life. And I hope I continue to have your support going forward, because I have many, many, many twisted tales to tell you.

Just flip the page and you'll get an idea of what I mean.

– Dimaro
October 29-30, 2021

SOLOMON "BIG POP" TOLES WILL RETURN

PHILIP TOLES II WILL RETURN

CLARLEN "THE BEAST IN THE NIGHT" WILL RETURN

SATURN CITY WILL RETURN

JAR JAR WILL RETURN

THE RED LADY WILL RETURN

SOLOMON "BIG POP" TOLES WILL RETURN

PHILIP TOLES II WILL RETURN

CLARLEN "THE BEAST IN THE NIGHT" WILL RETURN

SATURN CITY WILL RETURN

JAR JAR WILL RETURN

THE RED LADY WILL RETURN

Oo Pp Qq Rr Ss Tt Uu Vv Ww Xx

SOLOMON "BIG POP" TOLES WILL RETURN

PHILIP TOLES II WILL RETURN

ELAREEN "THE BEAST IN THE NIGHT" WILL RETURN

SATURN CITY WILL RETURN

JAR JAR WILL RETURN

THE RED LADY WILL RETURN

SOLOMON "BIG POP" TOLES WILL RETURN

PHILIP TOLES II WILL RETURN

ELAREEN "THE BEAST IN THE NIGHT" WILL RETURN

SATURN CITY WILL RETURN

JAR JAR WILL RETURN

THE RED LADY WILL RETURN

Manufactured by Amazon.ca
Bolton, ON

22685594R00107